RIDGERUNNERS

RIDGERUNNERS

MICKY NEILSON

Ridgerunners

Future House Publishing

ISBN: 978-1-944452-89-6

Developmental editing by Mackenzie Hendricks
Substantive and copy editing by Mandi Diaz
Proofreading by Kayla Echols
Interior design by Sara Ansted

ACKNOWLEDGMENTS

This book would not have been possible without, first and foremost, Cameron Dayton, for recommending me to Adam Sidwell. Many thanks, Brother Cam!

Also instrumental in the creation and execution of Ridgerunners was one of the smartest people I know, Andrew Ward. He helped me with the science every step of the way, and my gratitude cannot be overstated. (I am, after all, primarily a creative guy—a right brainer. Science fascinates me, but there are certainly times when it just makes my head hurt.) Finally, I would like to thank David Tulo for his assistance and support.

CHAPTER 1

Stations.

Clusters of research and development stations. That was what Captain Rowan Bartlett *should* have been looking at. Instead, the *Imperious's* panoramic floor-to-ceiling window offered an unobstructed view of Europa's swirling, terraformed atmosphere.

Bartlett ran a hand over his short, receding hair.

His chief mate stepped up next to him and wondered aloud, "If the stations were destroyed, where's the debris field?"

Bartlett quietly considered. Stealth tech? Certainly not far-fetched for the Europans. *But if so, why no communication?*

Silence could presage rebellion, but surely the Europans understood that war against the Collective was not a viable strategy, even for a civilization as advanced as theirs.

"Comms?" Bartlett called over his shoulder.

"Still nothing, sir," the communications officer answered.

Europa had ceased all communications with the Collective approximately sixteen hours ago. Bartlett's frigate, the *Imperious*, had been the closest company ship to Jupiter and its inhabited moons. They had tried to establish contact en route, yet not only had those attempts failed to yield results, but there had also been no challenge issued by the outer sentry rings when they arrived in Europan-occupied space.

Mainly because, as with the R&D stations, the sentry rings were simply *not there*.

An update had been sent to MARSA to be further relayed to Earth and the Collective headquarters. That news would *not* be well received.

The chief mate moved nearer the windows, as if a change in vantage point could produce for the naked eye what their scanners could not.

Bartlett turned back toward the operations deck, a raised, semicircular space around the captain's chair. His op crew sat at stations lining the walls to both sides of the bridge entry. As in all Collective designs, the modular hologram stations adhered strictly to the law of "form follows function" with one exception: scale. The executive-level belief being that size conveyed power.

Bartlett ordered, "Bring us into low orbit and give me a full spectrum sweep of the—"

"Sir, tracking an incoming object." This from the second

mate. "Distance one point nine kilometers, closing at eighty kilometers per second. Spherical in shape, approximately ninety-one centimeters in diameter."

"Shields up and go to code yellow," Bartlett replied.

"Shields up, sir," the third mate responded.

"Code yellow, aye." The chief mate jogged back to his station.

The second mate cut in, "Object's come to a full stop, one kilometer to port. Bearing 302.298."

"Give me something useful," Bartlett commanded.

"Scanning," the second mate answered. "Metallic. Tristeel. Low heat signature. Zero exhaust—"

"Can it put holes in us?" Bartlett asked. He was a military man, keen on threat assessment. He had a healthy fear of what Europan tech could do. Yet he was also a company man, and as such, his fear of next-gen weaponry paled in comparison to his fear of failure.

"No apparent weapons capabilities, sir. Looks like some kind of drone."

A drone? Just observing?

The third mate spoke quickly: "Secondary object inbound . . . just appeared . . . maybe from behind Europa?"

Bartlett rushed onto the op deck and over to the third mate's station, eyeing the sensor display where a pulsing red dot quickly closed distance.

"It's a ship," the young man continued. "Sigma class. Fusion drive. Shields active."

With a few quick taps over the third mate's shoulder, Bartlett raised a holographic tactical overview that hovered at a diagonal just in front of the captain's chair. He put one hand on the chair's back, observing the top-down view of his

3

own ship and the small drone dot out to the port side. He placed his fingers at the bottom right corner of the display and pinched. The tactical field of view widened to include the incoming ship.

The chief mate had joined him. "Vessel identifier?"

"Negative," the third mate answered. "I'm reading multiple vessel types."

Ridgerunners. Pirates. They prowled the outer reaches of the solar system, preying on cargo ships that ventured to the Jovian planets or the farposts or the asteroid belts, all collectively known as the *Ridge.* And thus, *Ridgerunners.*

But how were they using shield technology? Shield tech was still relatively new, developed by the Europans less than half a span ago . . . Were the pirates responsible for the Europans' disappearance? Had they stolen the shield tech and figured out how to use it? Or was this ship Europan, masquerading as pirate?

Bartlett punched a button on the arm of his chair, starting a transmission. "Incoming vessel, this is Captain Bartlett of the Collective ship *Imperious.* State your business or be fired upon."

Bartlett's message was greeted by silence. On the hologram, the incoming ship's dot stopped.

The third mate spoke, "They're readying weapons, starboard side."

"Code red. Ready all missiles, starboard side."

The weapons officer confirmed Bartlett's order as the chief mate rushed to his station and initiated the code red.

"Ship is coming about, but . . . port-side facing." The third mate sounded confused. And with good reason. Why in all the known worlds would a hostile ship ready weapons

4

on one side and turn to face their enemy with the opposite side?

"Lock missiles, confirm," Bartlett ordered.

The weapons officer confirmed.

Bartlett pressed a button on the chair to open all channels. "Unidentified vessel, respond immediately or be destroyed. This is your final warning."

After a few seconds of silence, Bartlett commanded: "Shields down."

"Shields down," the third mate confirmed.

"Fire."

Eight Cyclone-class missiles blasted from the *Imperious's* starboard ports. Bartlett watched the salvo's progress on his display while the entirety of the op crew did the same at their respective stations.

Bartlett's mouth dropped as the larger dot of the unidentified vessel disappeared, to be replaced by a smaller dot . . . *before* the missiles reached their target.

Bewildered, the second mate said, "The drone, sir, it moved. Relocated."

"That's impossible."

"Missiles aborted," the weapons officer reported. "They're showing no target within acquisition—"

"Vessel to port, one kilometer! Missile lock. Incoming!" the third mate shouted.

At the same time the second mate blurted: "Two more vessels coming from behind Europa—"

"Shields up! Shields—"

"Too late!"

The floor shuddered beneath him. Bartlett grasped the seat back for support and yelled, "Damage?"

5

"Busters, port side," the second mate replied.

"Busters" blasted apart a ship's outer shell and bulkheads to make way for "seekers"—pirate specialties—that would pinpoint and eradicate a vessel's shield processor.

"Breach in sector three. Shields nonfunctional," the chief mate reported. "Mobilizing repair crews."

The shields. Just as Bartlett had feared.

On Bartlett's display, a second missile salvo arced from the enemy vessel and raced to the frigate's aft. After another jarring impact that rattled Bartlett down to his bones, the navigation officer reported that their gravity thrusters had been obliterated.

The thrusters, Bartlett thought, but not the drive. The ship still maintained one G internally.

Bartlett worked through his options: no gravity thrusters meant no propulsion. Orientation thrusters, meant mainly for docking maneuvers, were not gravity driven but provided only minimal acceleration. Certainly not enough to make a getaway or quickly reorient. They could blindly loose all missiles on the port side, but with as close as the ship was now, those missiles would never get far enough from the *Imperious* to arm.

Most Ridgerunners preferred to disable and board their targets. They would salvage anything and everything and either sell the pilfered materials or use them to bolster their own vessels.

Bartlett knew that pirates did not take prisoners. Unless . . .

Unless it was who he thought it was: the Pack. His second mate had reported multiple vessels. The Pack was known to use one vessel as a decoy and attack with their remaining fleet.

Bartlett shouted to the chief mate: "Battle stations! Scramble ARTs to all access points. Prepare to repel hostiles."

"Aye," the officer replied, busily punching buttons and relaying orders into his comm.

Just then, a shadow blocked the observation window's ambient light. Bartlett turned to see a massive beta-class vessel crossing their bow.

"Fire all forward batteries!" the captain blurted, but even as the command was issued, he watched guns on the enemy ship send streams of plasma rounds to various points out of view.

"Forward batteries neutralized," the second mate confirmed quietly.

Bartlett's heart sank as the massive ship proceeded to the *Imperious's* starboard side, guns still blazing. He rushed to the op deck, hovering over the chief mate's shoulder, eyeing a bank of holographic screens. Throughout the ship, alarms sounded, emergency lights strobed, and noncombat personnel rushed to their respective stations and readied for the worst.

"Open comm to ARTs," the chief mate advised.

On one of the screens, Bartlett could see an Armed Response Team gathered around the airlock, railguns held ready. He couldn't help but be nervous about the guns being used on his ship. Though the railgun "smart slugs" were designed to detect the structural makeup of *Imperious's* bulkheads and fragment before impact, things didn't always work perfectly. A hull breach and loss of pressurization was a very real threat in the face of any boarding attack. In that event, a lightly armored pressure suit would be the only thing keeping the team members alive. Hopefully.

The ship rocked slightly. The team waited.

Further down the hallway, a circular section of bulkhead flew inward, colliding with the opposite wall and falling to the grated floor.

"What just happened there?" the chief mate asked. "Is that—"

A pirate in "jury rig" poked his head in and lobbed a small, spherical arc grenade up the passageway toward the ART. Before the grenade even had time to go off, a second pirate, also in a cobbled-together pressure suit, stepped into the corridor and raised a weapon with a fat disk at the end of a long barrel.

"ART 1, you have a breach aft," Bartlett yelled. "Repeat, breach aft! Engage! Engage!" He pounded the back of the chief mate's seat, helpless to intervene and, once again, confused. For an invading craft to seal and breach apart from an airlock wasn't unheard of, but he had believed it beyond the pirates' capability.

Just as ART 1 repositioned to acquire the enemy, the pirate activated his weapon. A flat, bluish plane of transparent energy spread out from the disk and partitioned the hall. ART 1 unleashed railgun fire, but the slugs didn't penetrate the shield. The pirate fired; the disk, along with its shield wall, shot down the passageway, its edges reconfiguring to the contours of the corridor as it caught and carried the arc grenade with it, then swept into the ART, stacking them up, sweeping them to the end of the hallway, where the mass of bodies prevented it from pushing any farther.

A second later the arc grenade detonated, but the barrier held fast. Body parts, pieces of armor, and blood all bombarded the shield wall.

Bartlett's mouth dropped open. The entire first response team was just . . . gone.

And where had they gotten a *repulsor gun*? Repulsor gun tech had evolved from shield tech. But it was incipient: again, Europan in origin, contracted by the Collective but, thus far, issued to very few combat personnel and still in the field testing stage.

On the screen, the pirate who had fired remained still as the disk flew back down the corridor, rejoining his weapon's barrel. Once the disk locked in place, the blood-coated barrier disappeared, sending droplets of blood and bits of metal and flesh to the floor.

Bartlett's attention shifted to the screen showing ART 2's position at the starboard airlock, second level.

The chief mate spoke into the comm: "ART 2, be aware the enemy has breached level three port side. ART 1 is . . . lost."

On the screen, ART 2 responded immediately. Bartlett followed their progress across multiple screens as they made their way toward the forward corridor that would take them across to the breach.

Just then, a camera feed caught Bartlett's attention. It displayed a second breach, aft of where ART 2 had just been. A second breach. ART 2 had rounded the first corner, moving to port. The captain watched as a stream of pirates rushed through the second level feed. These attackers used more conventional weaponry, mainly centrifugal sling guns, but they were rushing headlong toward ART 2's unprotected rear.

Bartlett shouted, "ART 2, you have hostiles incoming

on your six! Turn and engage!" He looked to his chief mate. "Shut the blast doors forward, port side, third level, and lock down all forward lifts."

The chief mate complied.

Bartlett prayed this would prevent the first pirate team, the one with the repulsor gun, from engaging ART 2 so that squad could face the second pirate threat.

His pulse thundered as he stared, unblinking, at the feeds. The second ART waited at the juncture of the starboard passage and forward cross-corridor. One of the men peeked around the corner as a grenade bounced down the hall.

Billowing smoke filled the screen. The voice of the ART leader crackled over the speaker at the chief mate's station: "I hear bootsteps! Ready! On my mark!"

Bartlett could just make out the team leader kneeling at the juncture, his squad formed around him, aiming down the corridor.

"Fire!" the leader yelled.

The team fired slugs into the smoke. Their salvo met with no response as the railguns reloaded.

"Stomping sounds," the team leader's voice reported.

Bartlett leaned in, squinting. A thick, massive shadow emerged from the fog—a Vulcan armored suit. It had a tri-barrel, tri-disk centrifugal sling gun for a right arm . . . aimed directly at the squad.

"Take cover!" the team leader ordered. A barrage of hypersonic rounds ripped apart a soldier who hadn't moved quick enough, then shredded the bulkhead behind him.

Bartlett's hopes withered.

"First pirate team has cut their way into the forward stairwell, Level Three," the chief mate observed, pointing to another screen.

Bartlett ground his teeth. They were running out of options. If that first team got off of level three . . . "Shut—shut the blast doors starboard side, level two forward."

The officer complied, but through the haze in the starboard camera feed, Bartlett watched as the pirate in the Vulcan armor stood at the threshold. The gun arm and a tree-trunk-sized left arm spread out to prevent the blast doors from closing. Pirates swept past, closing in on ART 2.

The level three feed showed pirates flowing into the stairwell from the corridor.

Bartlett's blood ran cold. That first pirate team was headed down to level two. ART 2 was about to get cut down in the crossfire. And there was nothing he could do but watch.

But even that option was removed when both camera feeds were shot out.

"Send a mayday," Bartlett called to the communications officer.

A second later, the reply that Bartlett had feared came back: "All outgoing signals jammed, sir."

"Of course," the captain responded. "Seal the bridge."

The chief mate complied. Alarms sounded throughout the operations area, and two-meter-thick tristeel blast doors closed off the bridge's entry.

Bartlett was heading back to his seat, ready to attempt communication with the pirates once again, when the chief mate announced that a data terminal on level five had been accessed.

"Incoming video, same terminal," the communications officer notified.

Bartlett was unsure what to expect as he returned to the chief mate's station and said, "Patch it through."

Seconds later, a larger screen hovered in front of the others. A female appeared there. She had removed her jury-rigged helmet to reveal rugged but attractive features. Her hair was shaved on one side, braided and beaded on the other. The terminal mic had been activated, and she began speaking. The chief mate switched on the feed's volume.

"Captain," she began. "Outgoing signals are jammed. You have no backup. This ship is ours. We're accessing oxygen conduits to the bridge now." The woman held up a canister.

There was no need for her to elaborate. The captain immediately recognized the lethal X4 gas.

The pirate lowered the canister, leaned in, and said, "Should I pipe this gas in, or do we discuss the terms of your surrender?"

CHAPTER 2

I t'll be quick and painless," Tarsigh said.

Aladhra turned from the *Imperious's* observation window to face him. He straightened, assuming what she had come to call his "authoritative stance." It would work on most. He was tall, with thick shoulder pads, bracers, and greaves combining to accentuate an already sturdy frame. His gray hair was pulled back, shaved on the sides. A tattoo adorned the right side of his neck and face; currently it was a dragon, its head glowering from the cheekbone. Most pirates who served under Captain Tarsigh's command would acquiesce to the authoritative stance.

Most.

Aladhra glared at him unflinchingly. That stance hadn't worked on her when she had been a little girl, and it certainly wasn't working now. "They met our demands. We're letting them go."

The dragon on Tarsigh's face shifted and moved down his neck, out of sight, only to be replaced by a cobra coiling into striking position on the right side of his jaw. "They're already loaded in the lifepods," he said. "All it takes is a few missiles."

Aladhra looked once again to the window and out at the thirty small vessels suspended against the stars. He always did this. She could feel her blood beginning to boil.

"The stakes are too high," Tarsigh continued. "We can't afford to—"

"We can't afford to BE them!" Aladhra shouted, spinning to face him again, pointing out the viewport. "We're better than this!"

"You'd jeopardize everything we just gained. For what? No one will know the truth," Tarsigh replied. "They'll say they escaped."

"*We'll* know!" Her fists were balled now, arms shaking. "Or are you so far gone that doesn't mean anything?"

Tarsigh's mouth twisted slightly. It was an expression she knew well: one of surrender.

To say that their relationship was complex would be an understatement. Tarsigh was, in so many respects, like a father to her. But a surrogate father; one only necessary because her real father had died when she was nine . . . left to die by none other than the man standing before her.

And it was this fact alone that settled most disputes between them. She knew that he was still trying, even after

15

all these spans, to regain her trust. It was a battle she had vowed on the day of her father's death that he would never win.

Tarsigh threw up his hands. "Okay," he said. "They've got enough oxygen to last until they clear jamming range. After that they can send a distress call. But I want you to know, I think this is a mistake."

Behind Tarsigh, a door slid open. On the other side, Striker waited silently, brown eyes darting back and forth, hands out like he was steadying himself. "Did we, uh . . . reach a conclusion?"

"Stand down on the missiles," Tarsigh said.

The wiry tech officer nodded. "Right, I'll tell Braxx. In that case, transport's ready."

There was a nervous flutter in Aladhra's stomach. It was the same flutter she had experienced when their flagship, *Vagabond*, had skipped from one side of the Collective frigate to the other.

She waited now inside the Ridgerunner transport, strapped into her seat. The small vessel had left the *Imperious* and was floating just outside the exosphere of Europa.

Aladhra knew that a skip sphere waited down there, two meters above the surface. She also knew that as long as the transport's gravity drive adjusted for their depth change in Europa's gravity well when they skipped, she should have nothing to worry about.

It was the *should* part that made her nervous. This

technology was still unfamiliar and largely untested. At least by the Pack.

One meter away, Tarsigh worked at the ship's controls. Behind the two of them sat four guards.

"Right," Tarsigh said. "Here we go."

Aladhra kept her eyes on the small viewport. One instant she was looking out at the *Imperious*; the next, a brief wave of nausea passed through her system and the ship groaned slightly. Light streamed in through the window, bright enough to shut her eyes.

"Ha ha!" Tarsigh burst. "Played hell with the instruments, but it worked."

"Glad you're having so much fun," Aladhra deadpanned.

"I never had a doubt," Striker said into their headpieces, not attempting to conceal his lie.

Tarsigh unstrapped and donned a pair of shade lenses. Aladhra and the guards did the same as the transport's ramp extended.

Tarsigh took a few steps from the craft onto the polished stone of the deserted courtyard and pivoted. He eyed the vessel, then looked up to the sky, neutral expression breaking into a wide grin. Aladhra walked out and stared skyward as a spectacular aurora rolled over them.

"I like this new technology," Tarsigh said brightly, looking at her now. "A welcome change, not to have to burn your way through an atmosphere."

Still angry at him, she offered no answer, instead lifting her gaze once again to what primitive men and women on Earth would have called the heavens. A beautiful sight, like standing beneath an ocean. On the heels of this thought came the sound of distant waves. Somewhere beyond this

17

massive platform, she knew, was a vast sea.

Tarsigh had already moved on. Aladhra reluctantly tore her attention away and joined the captain and guards. Together, they continued on to where a single open doorway waited in a low, nondescript building.

They made their way in, footsteps echoing across an expansive, gleaming entry; they strode down wide corridors that illuminated as they progressed, then carried on through one open doorway after another. The Europans had been as good as their word; the entirety of their operations complex was laid open to them. Now all that remained was to see if the grand prize awaited as promised.

The skip tech had been provided as a show of good faith. Even the Ridgerunners' most accomplished techs were largely confounded by it; it had taken Europan engineers to retrofit the Pack vessels with the required equipment and weave the necessary materials through the various ships and transports' hulls before the pirates could even hope to make use of it.

The Ridgerunners had then taken their leave, as requested, and when they returned, the Europans had departed, used that selfsame tech to hopscotch their way right out of the solar system, aiming to be the first colonists of some extrasolar planet. Before departing, they communicated to Tarsigh and Aladhra their wish that if the rest of humanity ever caught up to them, the Collective regime would be nothing but a distant memory.

And it was their oath to the Pack that whatever lay in the inner sanctum of the op complex would accomplish that very thing. Tarsigh had called the Europans heroes.

"Heroes are fools," Aladhra had said. And she had meant

it.

Throughout the Inter-Worlds War, the Collective had steadily gained power across the system, but pockets of resistance had held out, the greatest hub being on Mars.

It had been in the Red Planet's orbit, aboard a doomed rebel command and control sentry station named *Vig*ilant, that Aladhra's father, Cole, had died. Cole had confronted Collective saboteurs, buying time for Tarsigh and the other rebels to escape.

Her father had died a hero, Tarsigh had told her, time and again. As if that would make her feel better. It didn't. Better a selfish, alive father than a dead hero.

Her opinion had been firm since that time, and if anything, over the years it had only intensified: heroes were fools.

A hum of machinery accompanied their descent now as the six of them took a lift down three levels. They stepped out of the lift into a single long hallway with an open door and a darkened room at the end. Tarsigh shot Aladhra a look. This was it. Their prize, if it waited, waited in that room. The nervous flutter in Aladhra's stomach returned.

When they passed through the doorway, the room opened up to their left. It was a cavernous space, completely empty save for one single item: a black cube, roughly forty centimeters to a side, angular with pulsing lines of power.

The four approached and regarded the item silently. This, then, was the weapon provided against the Collective by the Europans:

A data cube.

CHAPTER 3

Aladhra strode into the Vagabond's meeting room two minutes early. Braxx sat on one side, bent over his tablet punching buttons. The six-foot-five goliath's ruddy beard bobbed up and down while he muttered to himself. Braxx was the Pack's armorer and smith, one of the only men capable of operating the Vulcan armor he himself had modified.

"Whatcha workin' on, Braxx?" she asked.

"'Tis a surprise, Ladhi," he answered, looking up and favoring her with a grin and a wink.

Although Aladhra forced everyone on board to call her by her first name, the big man, Papa Bear, was the only one allowed to use the shortened version "Ladhi."

Braxx scratched at his beard, just under a tattoo—a half circle with three arrows fanned out like sun rays—on his right cheek. This tattoo, unlike Tarsigh's roving tattoos, never moved. It was not his only tattoo, though. He also bore a permanent insignia on his right arm. It was a broadsword pointing downward behind a heater shield, the shield face decorated with stars representing Earth and the inhabited celestial bodies.

The rebel insignia.

Braxx had been there when Tarsigh had left Cole behind. It was for him that Aladhra put forth the effort to get along with Tarsigh, but unlike Braxx, who was easy-going and stayed out of her business, Tarsigh insisted on trying to replace her father.

Tarsigh entered the room and took his seat at the opposite end of the table. More of the command arrived shortly. Striker hopped into a chair and immediately put his boots on the table. The navigations officer, Findlay, sat next to him and shoved those boots off. As the communications officer took a spot next to Braxx, Striker socked Findlay in the shoulder.

Findlay struck back at Striker's arm, a blow which he casually wiped away.

"Oh, you'll have to do much better than that," Striker said.

Findlay was winding up for a harder swing when Tarsigh punched a button to transmit the proceedings to the Pack's five sub-captains on their respective ships and called the meeting to order.

"Next time," Findlay said.

Striker shook his head.

"I know you're waiting to hear what we brought back," Tarsigh began.

Aladhra was fairly certain that word of their prize had already spread among the crew. Word always traveled fast, even among all six ships in the Pack's fleet. And there had been plenty of time for the rumor mill to kick into high gear while the armada proceeded to open space a significant distance from Europa.

"What we have . . . is a data cube." He leaned in, tattoo-tentacles reaching up his neck. "Your next question might be: what's on it? But here's the cut . . . we don't know what's on it. And our tech wizard—" Tarsigh aimed his gaze at Striker, who shrugged. "—doesn't know how to retrieve what's on it. So where that leaves us is, we need to bring in someone. I've sent a message to Spirion Bak."

"What?" Aladhra sat bolt upright. "He's a liability," she blurted. "Either stupid or devious. Maybe both. All of which is dangerous."

The Pack had dealt with Spirion before, paying him to steal Collective shield codes that had been brand-new at the time. He had handed over three codes that proved to be useless within a cycle, keeping the remaining codes to sell to other Ridgerunners.

"He's a necessary evil. There's no one else to reach out to, so you'll need to trust me on this," Tarsigh said.

Before anyone else could interject, Braxx spoke up: "We'll keep a close watch on him. Meantime, I've a proposal . . ."

Aladhra bit her tongue, making a mental note to take the matter up again with Tarsigh once the meeting was over.

Braxx hit a button on the tablet, and a holographic metal plaque appeared and began rotating over the table. Engraved on it was the word "*Skipjack*."

"What's this?" Striker asked.

"My proposal," Braxx answered. "With this new tech, I thought maybe it was time to give our girl a new name. This is what I came up with."

Skipjack . . . it had character. She had liked *Vagabond*, but she had to admit this was better.

Tarsigh sat back, rubbing his chin. "Okay," he said. "We'll vote on it. All in favor of renaming *Vagabond* to *Skipjack*?"

Tarsigh said "Aye." Around the table then, one by one, the command crew answered. Each replied "aye," finishing with Aladhra. When they had spoken, the five sub-captains replied "aye" over the comm.

"The 'ayes' have it," Tarsigh said, spreading his arms wide and calling out loudly, "*Vagabon*d, I hereby rechristen thee *Skipjack*!"

CHAPTER 4

Grant Hollingsworth glanced at the time, the glowing numbers displayed through a subcutaneous implant in his wrist. He had five minutes. The meeting he had just come from—chairing the committee to form a committee on phase four asteroid mining—had been an important one. But where he was going now was far more important.

This was the moment Grant had waited three spans for. Promotion. Why else would Brenn Condon, Vice President of Special Operations and Emerging Technologies, grant him access to the executive lift, invite him all the way to the top floor?

His gaze traveled upward, above the lift doors to the

Collective's number one core value, engraved in the metal in bold, harsh letters: FAILURE IS DEATH.

Grant smiled. Failure. He didn't know the meaning of the word. Still . . . he pressed on his wrist to get a readout of his pulse. 110.

He took a deep breath and exhaled, reached into his pocket, and pulled out a pill box. Inside were all sorts of pick-me-ups and even-me-outs. He grabbed a Zentazine and popped it as the lift's upward momentum ceased.

The doors opened to reveal a short hallway. Adjusting his suit, Grant stepped out and across to the closed double doors with Condon's name in glowing holographic font. He knocked once.

"Enter!" a man's voice commanded.

Grant did as he was bidden. Condon's desk was situated facing the door, and the man himself sat behind it, hands clasped on its top. His short hair was meticulously styled, not a single strand out of place. Though the vice president was not a particularly large man, the thick muscles of his biceps and deltoids strained against his suit jacket's synth-weave. His stern features remained as unreadable as ever, and Grant noted that the windows at the rear of the room that faced Upper Los Angeles were currently blacked out.

Sitting stiffly in a chair fronting the desk was Grant's boss, Chen. To Grant's immediate right, seated with her back against the wall, was Danique.

HR.

Hopefully the Zentazine was kicking in now. HR always made Grant nervous. Danique was a thin woman with black hair pulled back so tight it made the veins in her forehead stand out. When he met the woman's gaze, her eyes bored into the depths of his soul. Whether or not she approved of what she saw there was anyone's guess.

Her presence here was certainly to be expected for a promotion. She would need to talk to him about his raise in salary, increased profit sharing, etc. Reassured, Grant took a seat directly across the desk from Condon and did his best to appear casual, calm, and confident.

Condon stared for a moment at the digital docs on the desktop, angled just enough that Grant couldn't see. "Mr. Hollingsworth," Condon began, "among your many responsibilities, you serve as liaison between the Collective and the Europan Research and Development Directorate, correct?"

"Yes," Grant answered tentatively.

Why was Condon asking a question he already knew the answer to?

"And how do you feel that's going?" Condon continued in an even tone.

Grant felt suddenly uncomfortable. That particular question was *always* a loaded one.

"It's been good," Grant answered, glancing to his left at Chen, trying to get a read. "All of their current projects are on track for—"

"I take it you impressed upon the Europans that a synergistic relationship with us was in their best interests?"

"Yes, I made it clear—"

"That any breach of trust would have repercussions," Condon pressed.

"Yes! Why, what's happened?"

"Europa has ceased all contact," the vice president explained. "We sent a company ship—they messaged that the outer sentry rings were not even there. Neither were the orbiting research and development stations." Condon lifted his hands and wiggled his fingers. "Gone," he said. "Vanished."

Grant looked to Danique, whose gaze continued to drill into him.

Condon went on: "That ship, the *Imperious*, was then attacked. By Ridgerunners."

Grant's blood turned cold. This was not going well . . . not going well at all.

Condon continued: "The ship was boarded and seized. Using *Europan* technology!" Though he accentuated those last words, his voice increased only slightly in volume. "What's left of the crew is floating in orbit, in lifepods, awaiting rescue."

"Well, of course, I had no idea—"

"The Collective is a machine. We are all parts in that machine. When one part fails, the machine breaks down. This was a *catastrophic* failure."

Grant leaned forward, head scanning quickly from one side to the other. "Don't think that I can't see what you're doing here," he said.

"Is there someone else we should be looking at?" Danique asked. "Some failure elsewhere?"

"What? No—"

"You admit then that Europa is your responsibility," Chen added.

"I see what's happening. Your neck is on the line, so you're throwing me to the wolves," Grant argued. He stood, and when he did, Danique was somehow already standing, blocking his way.

"Retake your seat, Mister Hollingsworth," she said.

He obeyed.

Danique glanced down at her data pad and typed something one handed. Condon looked down at his desk readout, then to Danique, and nodded.

"You're hereby terminated, Mister Hollingsworth," Condon said. "Effective immediately."

Danique reached down and turned over Grant's right hand. She swept a device over his arm that deactivated the access chip implanted in his wrist.

"Arrangements will be made to have your things sent to you," Condon stated.

"I gave fifteen years of my life to this," Grant said.

Danique was pulling him up by the arm now. "Time to go," she said.

This couldn't be happening. What would his wife think? What about his kids?

"Go where? What am I supposed to—"

Chen grabbed his other arm and helped Danique to usher him out.

"It's not right! You hear me?" he continued to protest as they led him into the hall.

Danique and Chen flanked Grant to the lift, each of them holding one of his arms. Danique pressed the button, and when the car arrived, they let go.

Grant entered. "What happens now?" But when he turned, the other two were still in the hall, regarding him with those same flat expressions as the lift doors closed. "What is this?" he yelled.

The lift sped down twenty-two floors to the lobby, passed that, and dropped down into the subbasement levels . . . then down *further*, beyond where Grant knew any more floors to exist, before the car finally came to rest.

He looked to the doors. He hit the button to open them, but nothing happened. The Zentazine was doing nothing to calm his raging pulse. Sweat beaded on his forehead and ran into his eyes.

There was a hum of machinery as the walls and floor began to vibrate. He stepped to the doors, put his fingers to the seam where the doors met, and tried to pull them apart. He stepped back and pounded on them. "Hey! HELP!" he yelled. His heart was a piston inside his chest.

He hit the red emergency button.

No response.

Then, suddenly, it felt as if he were falling . . . up and backward. His brain struggled to make sense of the disorientation as he realized he was floating in the center of the elevator.

It was then that he felt the compression, and he put together with horrific clarity just what was happening: a point source of gravity had been created in the car's center, and the pull of that gravity was increasing. A memory flashed through his mind of engineers overheard one day in the cafeteria, theorizing that playing with gravity in such a way could be an effective method of . . . killing someone. Grant's heart pounded furiously. As he flailed in a blind panic, his legs suddenly bent; his arms flung back and behind him; his head and back arched. He screamed as his body began to curl like a closing fist. Electric, white-hot pain swept through him. His screams ended with the shredding of his lungs.

Roughly thirty seconds later, his self-awareness ceased altogether.

CHAPTER 5

B renn Condon ran through a myriad of potential scenarios as the shuttlecar carried him higher, towards the Old Man's low Earth orbit executive suite.

He played out every possible conversation, accusation, and interrogative that might be leveled at him—"How is it you didn't see this coming?" "It's time to scale back your responsibilities so you can regain focus"—and he rehearsed various appropriate responses for each and every one. He had already begun manufacturing a narrative painting Grant as a burnout who had succumbed to stress. If the Old Man tried to demote him, Condon would attempt a riskier gambit: implicating Grant as a traitor and inciting fear that other moles may exist while simultaneously reaffirming his own loyalty.

The shuttlecar docked at last. Condon exited the vehicle directly into the short foyer of the suite. He was within five feet of the door when it opened automatically.

The suite was circular, with a large window array bounding half of the disk-shaped room. The slanted glass allowed an unparalleled view of the world below, a vista that was particularly breathtaking now as the mobile suite passed over China. It wasn't, however, the scenery that galvanized Condon. It was the station, the elevation above all others. It was a view that Condon meant to have as his own.

The Old Man was stooped, leaning against the glass, staring out. He was known by a few different names, including Pindl Folk, and at one time, the Miracle Boy. A field trip for young Folk and his classmates—some of Earth's most promising, ambitious, and intelligent young academics—had turned deadly when their transport crashed on Mars while en route to Utopia Planitia. Everyone on board had died, except for Folk. And thus, the moniker of Miracle Boy had been assigned to him.

Truth be told, Condon didn't hold many people in high esteem. Even to him, however, Folk was something of an icon. He was chairman of the Collective board and for many, the public face of the company. Largely because of the PR that had resulted from his close shave with death, he embodied the idyllic symbol of a man who had faced the impossible and had come out on top. A fighter. A survivor—an image that Folk had leveraged to great advantage throughout his immensely successful and illustrious career.

Condon gave the room a quick scan to see if Danique was present. She wasn't, which was a relief. There was another woman, however, sitting at one of two chairs in front of Folk's oval-shaped desk. She glanced over her shoulder and smiled tightly.

"Hello, Brenn," the Old Man said gruffly without turning around. "You know Belinda Bullock? VP of Strategic Planning and Advanced Initiatives?"

Condon had heard the name but had no idea what her title meant. Nobody did. Then again, nobody knew what half the VP titles meant. Rumors swirled that Strategic Planning and Advanced Initiative's purview was beyond top-secret projects, mostly bio-engineering and enhancement.

"We haven't met," he replied, crossing to her seat with his hand extended.

She stood and gave a firm shake. "Now we have," she said, her expression carefully guarded.

Folk turned to face them. Condon thought he had aged quite a bit since the last time they had spoken. He had met three times face-to-face with Folk over the last cycle and each time the CEO looked worse than before. The Old Man never spoke of it, but rumors of his failing health had been circulating for a while. He had lived a long, vibrant life of nearly one hundred and fifty years, but his bio-enhancements had taken him about as far as the current technology allowed. Money, it seemed, couldn't buy *everything*.

"A shame about your man . . . Hollis?" the Old Man commented.

"Hollingsworth," Condon said. "Grant."

"Good, though, that he assumed proper responsibility.

I wouldn't relish the conversation we'd be having had the blame fallen on you."

Condon was relieved that his stratagem of discrediting Grant had been successful. It wouldn't surprise him if the Old Man suspected his machinations, but it also stood to reason that the CEO would respect such maneuvering. After all, it had been Folk himself who had taught Condon to always have a backup. Always leave a way out.

"As you said, the important thing is he accepted responsibility . . . and we did what was best for the—"

Folk coughed once, twice; then his skin turned a faint reddish color as the two preliminary coughs evolved into a small hacking fit. At one point he leaned slightly over and Condon wondered if he would vomit.

"Sir, are you—" he began, but the Old Man waved him off.

It took another moment for Folk to regain full composure. With that accomplished, he held a hand toward the chairs and said, "Sit, sit."

Bullock and Condon both complied.

Folk walked slowly, carefully, around and placed two hands on the back of his chair. "I just received word," he said, "That Dane Koros has been captured."

"That's great news," Condon replied.

There were a large number of pirate groups throughout the solar system. In the beginning, these had been comprised almost entirely of former rebels. Over time that changed; first, more and more of the criminal-minded came to realize the lucrative nature of piracy and adopted the practice, and second, more and more of the prior rebels were captured and executed—a process that Condon took great pleasure in witnessing and, whenever possible, contributing to. Pirates were exceedingly dangerous because they were unpredictable and for the most part, uncontrollable. The war veterans were the worst because they were experienced and familiar with Collective military tactics. Koros and his so-called "Old Guard" and Tarsigh and his "Pack" were all that remained of the rebel variety of pirates, as far as anyone knew.

"Unfortunately, he doesn't seem to know the whereabouts of Tarsigh or the Pack," Folk said. "But under extensive neural probing he did reveal a name—a member of their support network. Customs officer at MARSA. One Karl Redding."

MARS-A was the red planet's first orbiting station. Some imaginative genius at some point decided to just start calling it MARSA and, unfortunately, the name had stuck.

"I see," Condon said.

Bullock remained silent.

"I take it Redding is not yet in custody?" Condon asked.

Folk walked carefully around his chair and sat with a small groan, then smiled and said, "Not yet."

Condon knew better than to ask why. The Old Man would get around to explaining in his own time.

Finally, Folk said, "We had a deal with the Europans. A pact. And they have broken that pact. The fact that Tarsigh and his Pack are now in possession of their new technology is a problem. I want you and Belinda to work together to find a solution."

What was this? Condon looked over at Bullock, who gave him no more than a sideways glance. The Old Man didn't do anything without reason. So why partner them up?

And then it struck him: what if this meant that he and Bullock were in line to take Folk's position when the Old

Man finally retired or kicked off? This could be a test to see which of them measured up.

Folk continued: "You may find that the information regarding Redding will prove useful in this regard. Whatever the case, I encourage you to be as . . . creative as necessary. In the meantime, Koros will face trial and a subsequent execution."

Condon nodded, with only the slightest hesitation. He turned to Bullock and said, "Well then, it seems you and I should put our heads together."

CHAPTER 6

Aladhra glared at Spirion, the weasel that Tarsigh had decided to bring in for the cube.

Spirion ignored her and ran a hand through his greasy black hair while punching more buttons on his data pad. "At least they left you an adaptor," he said.

Tarsigh, Aladhra, and Striker were clustered in the engineering bay, waiting for their "guest" to finish his analysis. Aladhra could feel the vibration of the gravity drive in the floor, could hear its thrum behind the barred doors to their rear. The bay was fairly open, with terminals along the aft bulkhead and pipes and conduits at the fore. Braxx paced back and forth in front of the open doorway opposite where the others stood. In the middle of the room, Spirion pursed his lips, regarding the data cube at his feet.

Aladhra continued watching him. His condition for meeting on their ship was that none of them be armed. Most likely because he feared reprisal for his former treachery—still, she didn't trust the man.

The cube sat in what they all assumed was the adaptor—a softly glowing base.

"Our stuff and their stuff won't play nice without it." Spirion squatted down, bony knees poking at the fabric of his baggy pants. "Lot o' data here. Let's unpack a cluster and see what we got . . ."

He stood as a hologram table of numerous named files appeared above the cube. "Here we go." He reached out and tapped one of the files, causing a holographic document to hover just in front of his face. "Ship manifest. From eleven spans ago," he said, scrutinizing. "Biohazardous material . . . the *Steadfast*. Collective ship. It was bound for the colony of Providence on Enceladus."

"That's where the outbreak of Black Pox first occurred," Aladhra thought aloud. "Before it spread to Mars."

"And before the vaccinations," Tarsigh added, "that netted the Collective billions in chits."

Spirion opened another file, swiping through multiple holographic docs. "Lab records, routing logs, date and time-stamped deliveries . . . this is Slipstream."

Aladhra had heard plenty of Slipstream—it was an illegal, lethally addictive drug that caused hallucinations and made users feel as if they had slipped into an alternate reality or past.

"What we've got here," Spirion continued, "is a supply

and distribution chain for the drug . . . and it's got Collective fingerprints all over it. This is crazy. Based on what I'm seeing so far, this entire cube is filled with the Collective's . . . dirty laundry, to use an old Earth term." For a moment, Spirion seemed to be lost to his own thoughts.

He reached down and pressed a button on his belt, then clicked his heels together. Blue lights illuminated on the sides of his shoes. He then squatted down, grabbing onto the cube and adaptor. Suddenly Braxx, Tarsigh, Striker, and Aladhra were overtaken by a sensation of falling from a great height, as they flew sideways across the floor to the piping along the bulkhead at the end of the room. All loose items in the room set to motion as well, sliding or scudding to the same wall. A torque wrench clanged and bounced off a conduit just centimeters from Striker's head.

"The boots and other accoutrements are a little something I've been working on," Spirion announced proudly. "They reorient the gravity around them."

"It really has been a pleasure doing business," Spirion remarked as he stepped through the doorway and into the corridor heading back to the docking bay.

"You were supposed to check him!" Tarsigh barked from his awkward position between two large pipes.

"How could I have known about the boots?" Striker yelled back. He was moving slowly, probably trying to detect if any bones had been broken.

"Who cares?" Aladhra blurted. "Spirion's getting away with the cube!" She was sore, and the muscles especially in her back had seized. She forced the locked-up sinews into motion and managed to get to her feet. When she did, she was standing on a cluster of conduits, her body jutting out parallel to the floor. It was as if the room had been turned on end; as if the *Skipjack* had tipped onto its nose like a sinking ship. It took an instant for her brain to adjust to the spatial disorientation.

Tarsigh retrieved an earpiece from his overcoat pocket and positioned it on his right ear. "This is Tarsigh, can anyone hear me?" He waited a second and said, "Anyone on board *Skipjack*, respond." He looked at Aladhra and shook his head. "Nothing," he said. "You can bet he's jamming ship-to-ship communication also."

"Braxx, come here," Aladhra said.

Luckily the big man had been close to the fore bulkhead when gravity had been altered. He groaned, crawling along two large pipes to get to where Aladhra was standing. Once there, he maneuvered to a standing position as well.

Aladhra's eyes ran up to the room's entrance. It was the nature of Ridgerunner vessels that they were cobbled together, their interior design imprecise, not at all like the neat and orderly Collective vessels with a place for everything and everything in its place. In the *Skipjack's* engineering room, on this side of the access door, cables and conduits hung from the ceiling and ran along the bulkhead to the end of the room where they connected to data terminals.

"Stand against the wall," she told Braxx.

"Which wall?" he asked.

Aladhra reached over and indicated the bulkhead housing the entrance.

The bulky man did as she asked, his girth resting against the tristeel.

"What are you on to?" Tarsigh asked, now standing as well.

"Gonna have to climb," Aladhra answered. "All those times Dad, and then you, told me to stop climbing on everything . . . well, now that's gonna come in handy."

Braxx held his hands interlaced in front of him to give Aladhra a boost.

"Not sure this is a good idea," Tarsigh said.

"Wasn't asking," Aladhra replied. She stepped into Braxx's hands and then up onto his shoulders. The two of them were now stacked sideways on the wall.

From Braxx's shoulders, Aladhra leapt, her fingers grasping onto the entranceway's frame. She pulled her upper body onto it and then maneuvered to where she could stand on the thick jamb. She gained her footing and stretched, her fingertips barely touching the inner frame on the other side. She hopped and grabbed onto the outside edge of the jutting metal, hoisting herself to where she could lay her forearms on the frame, kicking her feet in the open doorway. She reached out for the cables, grabbed on, and continued her climb, arms burning now and her fingers weakening. The data terminals were just a few meters away.

Standing on the frame, she grabbed a knife from her side and jammed it at waist height between two cables near a brace mounting the conduits to the wall. She climbed further, using the knife handle as a foothold, pushing herself on, grasping higher on the cables, sweating now, fingers reaching for the nearest terminal . . .

The knife slipped and hurtled end over end. Tarsigh stepped to one side as Braxx dove, the knife missing his right leg by a centimeter. Aladhra dangled precariously from one hand for a breathless instant, her feet unmoored. If she fell now, the impact would break her legs at the very least.

She managed to rest the toe of her boot on the cable brace, enough to take on her weight so she could stretch out with her right hand to the terminal.

"Tell me what to do," she called to Striker.

He complied, issuing commands. Aladhra's grip began to fail as she rapidly punched buttons, completing the series of actions necessary to reorient the gravity that had been affected by Spirion's apparatus. With a final click, her grasp at last gave out and she fell, not to the other end of the room but down less than a meter to the cold floor.

At the room's opposite end, Braxx, Striker, and Tarsigh dropped as well.

"You're okay?" Tarsigh enquired to Aladhra, limping his way to her.

"Fine," she answered, holding up a hand to keep him at arm's length.

Seconds later a quick look in the docking bay confirmed that Spirion's ship was gone. They hurried as quickly as they could toward the bridge, and Tarsigh blurted into his headset, "This is the captain, is anyone hearing me?" Then, to Striker, as they came to a corridor intersection, "Get me one of the special drones, quick as you can!"

Without a word, Striker moved to obey.

"Comms are still jammed," Tarsigh announced as they entered command and control.

Aladhra made straight for her work station on the port side and just behind the raised area that hosted the captain's chair. The bridge could be cramped at times, not nearly as spacious as that of the bigger vessels like the *Imperious*, but it was one of the places Aladhra felt most at home.

"Did gravity go sideways in here?" Tarsigh asked,

drawing confused looks.

"Must have been outside the radius," Braxx said.

"Mm." Hitting buttons on the captain's seat arm, Tarsigh called up a holographic tactical display. "Scan for Spirion's cruiser," he ordered.

"Already on it," Aladhra said.

"Anyone care to fill me in?" Findlay asked from his navigation station.

Striker rushed in, holding an active spherical drone similar in size to one of Earth's old volleyballs. "Cruiser's out of range," Aladhra called, staring at the newly-arrived drone. "The data cube . . . it has skip tech?"

"I think so," Tarsigh answered. "Striker, see what you can do." Striker rushed to his station. "Hurry!" the captain added.

"It's locked on . . . the cube. I think," Striker reported seconds later.

"Is it the cube or not?" Tarsigh pressed.

Striker answered, "I'm still learning this tech, but . . . yes. It says it's reading the cube. Nearly out of range, though."

Tarsigh crossed to where the ball was resting on the floor and pressed a button; beeping noises now issued from the orb at decreasing intervals. "I hope you're right," the captain answered.

A second later, the drone turned to dark energy, a force that expanded into the shape and size of a forty-centimeter cube.

———•———

On board his cruiser, *Terminus*, Spirion had the ship on autopilot. He was inside a large space near the cargo hold, one he had modified to be his tech work area, and he had just removed the cube from the adaptor. There was something about the cube—something strange. And in order to get a better look, he had needed to get the adaptor out of the way. He knelt, leaning in, holding up a scanner that began detecting the cube's various metallic and electronic components. There was something . . . something that he had never seen on any other data cube, and that he couldn't readily identify. He looked at the scan. Whatever this mysterious material was, it was fully integrated into the—

Just then, there was a popping sound and a small rush of air as the cube simply disappeared, replaced by a sphere. One that was beeping . . .

Rapidly.

It was a familiar sound. Spirion sprang up, took two running steps and jumped onto the nearby work table, pulling it over with him, forming a shield as the orb exploded with a tremendous, blinding flash.

CHAPTER 7

Following Condon and Bullock's meeting with the Old Man, the two of them proceeded directly to one of Earth Collective HQ's many conference rooms. Bullock sat at the head of the small table. Refusing to sit in an inferior position, he elected to remain standing, pacing along one side.

"What are your thoughts?" she asked.

"I should think that's obvious," he answered. "We subject Karl Redding to neural probing and extract as much information as possible. Then we try him as a seditionist."

"I have it on good authority that operators such as Redding communicate with Ridgerunners beneath a veil of anonymity and obscurity," Bullock said. "Specifically to prevent identification and tracking if any member of their network is caught."

Condon wondered where she was getting her intelligence.

Bullock continued: "I think a better plan would be to dangle a carrot—immunity to prosecution in exchange for spreading word through whatever encrypted channels he uses—that we've placed a bounty on the Pack."

"A bounty?"

"One billion chits. The one and only thing that can be counted on with pirates is that they're greedy. So we *use* that greed. Use them to do our work for us."

Condon considered. Currency *was* one way to control pirates. . . and they could, of course, announce such a bounty without channeling it through Redding by simply broadcasting it via the ISNN, but Condon knew—as did Bullock, apparently—that the Old Man would want to limit the number of hands this new Europan tech could potentially fall into. And though he hated to admit that Bullock was right, there was no denying it: pirates were exceedingly greedy. The only ones likely to choose the tech over the bounty were the ones who currently possessed it: the Pack.

"What's to prevent Redding from sending a warning to the Pack instead that we're after them?"

"They have the tech; they *know* we're after them. Redding has plenty of incentive to look after his own welfare."

"And who'll convince the Old Man to sign off on a one billion-chit payout?"

"I will," Bullock said without hesitation.

Condon weighed the proposal. If Bullock's plan failed, he could fairly easily place the blame at her feet and continue on with his own. If it succeeded, he could at least take partial credit . . . but that wasn't good enough. He needed to put his own stamp on it. Something he could point to that Folk would appreciate. An idea came to him, but for the time being, he kept it to himself.

Not long after, the two of them boarded the Collective Corvette *Spearhead*, accompanied by a rotating fighter escort bound for MARSA. Before setting off, Bullock had made good on her word by getting Folk's blessing on the proposed bounty. Condon was surprised, but then again, he was also certain the Old Man had weighed the risk versus reward and found the initiative worth greenlighting.

Upon landing at MARSA, Bullock and Condon pulled Redding from his post overseeing the cargo scanning and convened a meeting in a conference room above the docking bay. Two Collective enforcers accompanied them, should Redding attempt anything foolish—be that fight *or* flight.

Condon stood now at an observation window overlooking Docking Bay Seven, simultaneously feigning interest in the cargo vessel currently being unloaded and listening intently to Bullock laying out a very specific offer to Karl Redding.

When Bullock finished outlining her proposal, Condon waited patiently for Redding's response.

"What you're suggesting could get me killed," the man finally said.

Before Bullock could answer, the customs officer received a call. Condon turned slightly as Redding pressed a button on his wrist and stared at a rectangular lens over his left eye.

Redding licked his lips, said he would call the person back and ended the transmission.

"Your son?" Bullock asked.

Condon turned fully around. Redding's face had gone white.

"What—"

"Kyle, isn't it?" Bullock moved to Redding's desk, pressed a button on a holographic base; a three-dimensional image of a smiling young boy flickered into view.

Redding shrunk into his seat.

Condon thought about Bullock's previous words: "He has plenty of incentive to look after his own welfare." She had known about the boy and opted not to share that information. He cursed himself for not coming up with that leverage on his own. It was a novice mistake. Unacceptable.

"If you cooperate and we take the Pack into custody, there will be no threat to your son." The fact that Bullock didn't specify whether the suggested threat would come from the Pack or from the Collective wasn't lost on Condon, and most likely it wasn't lost on Redding.

The officer slumped silently, weighing his options, rubbing his balding head. Finally, he reached his decision. "Okay," he said. "Okay, I'll do it."

"How long to get the message out?" Condon asked.

"It'll be sent from here via tight-beam to all the relays throughout the system, with the usual time delays."

"Our associates will remain." Bullock indicated the security detail. "And inform us once the message is sent. Thank you for your time, Mister Redding."

Condon walked ahead of Bullock out of the office, through a corridor and out into the bustling terminal. He wished to speak to her about the information she had withheld, but before he turned around an automated voice in his earpiece informed him of a message. A second later, Bullock's voice was in his ear: "I'll meet you at departure in two hours."

Condon pivoted to address her directly, only to find that his "partner" was gone.

The adaptor was missing.

Aladhra and everyone else on the bridge looked at Striker, who gazed down at the cube in his hands. "Well . . . aside from the adaptor's absence, it appears to be okay."

Tarsigh sighed, while on the right side of his face and neck, the dragon dove down to be replaced by a roaring tiger. Aladhra could guess what he was thinking: that adaptor was the key to unlocking the rest of what the box possessed. Once they knew all of what was on the cube, they could, hopefully, intelligently figure out the best way to use it.

"How tough will it be to get a new one?" Aladhra asked.

"Well, it's a very specialized piece of equipment," Striker replied.

"Any chance Spirion mighta' lived?" Braxx asked from his station.

"Hard to say," Tarsigh responded, leaning against the back of his captain's chair. "Even if he did, we have no way of finding him, and the adaptor might very well have been destroyed in the explosion."

"I've got some connections," Striker offered. "I'll reach out." Tarsigh nodded, and the tech officer exited the bridge, taking the cube with him.

Before Tarsigh could take his seat, the communications officer, Gungan, said, "Sir, a news broadcast. You may wish to be aware." The large, dark-skinned man had hardly turned in his seat. His statement was characteristically terse, and as always, his expressionless face offered no hint as to whether the news might be good or bad.

The monitor closest to Tarsigh powered on, and he turned to see an ISNN anchor. "I repeat, we have just learned that Dane Koros, pirate, Ridgerunner, and former rebel, has been captured by the Collective. No additional information has been made available at this time, but rest assured—"

Aladhra's heart sank as she took in the holo-image of the pirate captain floating just beside the news anchor. Many spans ago, Koros had been the captain of the rebel ship *Redoubt*, the vessel that had carried Tarsigh, Braxx, and other insurgents to safety while Aladhra's father had stayed on board the *Vigilant*. Stayed, and died.

"Command meeting in twenty minutes," Tarsigh said.

When they all gathered in the meeting room twenty minutes later, Tarsigh wasted no time in getting straight to the point:

"We're all aware now of Dane Koros's capture," he began, shifting his gaze first to Braxx, then to Aladhra. "We can be certain he's been probed," the captain continued. "But we've had no contact with him in several spans, so we can be equally certain that the suits haven't extracted anything that will lead him back to us."

"Trial's next, then?" Braxx asked in a low voice.

"Imagine so," Tarsigh confirmed. "Don't be surprised if our names come up." He looked squarely at Braxx when he said this, and something passed across his features that Aladhra had trouble deciphering. Braxx looked at her and then looked quickly away.

"We've already been branded seditionists," Braxx said. "A charge punishable by death. The suits can pile on all the evidence they want. If they catch me, they'll still only kill me once."

Striker and Findlay chuckled. Aladhra smiled. She didn't always share the gallows humor of her compatriots, but she thought it was funny that *they* thought it was funny.

Tarsigh turned his attention to Striker. "I'm hoping you have good news about the adaptor."

"Got word just a few minutes ago," the tech officer answered. "My guy Garth says he has one. But he's jumpy, won't bring it to the ship. Wants to meet at Staryard Enc-1."

Aladhra had heard of it but never been there: Staryard Enc-1 floated in orbit outside Saturn's sixth largest moon, Enceladus. It performed maintenance and repair on all but the largest-class vessels.

She knew that neither the *Skipjack* nor any of the other major Pack ships could get near the yard without setting off Collective alerts. Luckily, the Pack had a few cruiser ships, purchased under false identities, that could pass screening and ferry a small contingent to the yard.

"Have you learned enough to skip us there?" the captain asked.

"I think so," Striker replied. "It's mainly an energy problem, but this far from the sun it should be minimal."

"Good. We'll skip the Pack in just out of scanner range

and take one of the cruisers," Tarsigh said. "Well, not 'we.' I'll be sitting this one out." He looked to Braxx. "As will you."

"We know," Striker interrupted. "Facial recognition. It'll have to be those of us whose pretty faces *aren't* in the system. Luckily, that's me, so I'll go. Good thing, too, since I'm the only one Garth trusts."

"I'll go, too," Aladhra said.

Tarsigh opened his mouth to say something, but she pointed a finger at him, stopping the words before they were uttered.

"Gungan, I want you to be my ears here," Tarsigh said instead. The stone-faced man nodded.

"I'm going!" Findlay blurted. "I never get to go. Anywhere."

"And what if the *Skipjack* needs its navigator?" Tarsigh asked.

"I'll find a suitable sub," Findlay added. "Please? I've got someone in mind."

"Who?"

"Jepps," Findlay answered.

Aladhra had spoken to Jepps on a few occasions. He was a dark-skinned first-generation Martian. The command team was all Earth born, except for Aladhra, whose mother had delivered her on board a space station orbiting Titan and died shortly after. The rest of the Pack was from different colonies throughout the system—diverse in background and culture but united in their hatred for the Collective regime. As for Jepps, the tall young man was wet behind the ears, but he had impressed her as dedicated and itching to prove his worth.

Tarsigh scrunched his lips and looked to Striker. "You can walk Jepps through skip tech, in case we need a quick exit?"

Striker nodded.

"And you trust Garth to deliver?"

"I do," Striker answered. "He has a reputation to maintain."

The cobra on Tarsigh's jaw relaxed, slithering into his shirt. "Fine, it'll be the three of you then. Let's make it happen," he said as the dragon crawled up his neck.

CHAPTER 8

Condon found a wall to lean against and, using a lens similar to the one used by Redding to speak with his son, skimmed through his never-ending backlog of messages. Afterward, he found himself wandering through a section of MARSA that boasted over half of its many restaurants. He had been mulling over an idea and decided now on a course of action. Standing at the bar of an upscale astropub called Red Devil, he put in a call to the MARSA liaison.

"Get me the highest level Collective tech on site," he said.

He was given the name Kent Stephenson and put

through. Condon spent the next few minutes explaining what it was he wanted, and had just finished when he heard his name called. Looking to his left, he spotted an old classmate, Jenny Cooper, taking a seat at the bar. Knowing he had an hour to kill before departure, he sat next to her.

She smiled, a gesture that Condon returned with his own practiced, tight-lipped acknowledgment.

"Still working out, I see," she said, eyeing his shoulders.

"Every other morning," he replied. It was a ritual he had begun in college. Not for health reasons—Condon was a "designer baby," meaning all unwanted, undesirable traits had been eliminated at the embryonic stage through genetic engineering. No, he engaged in his physical fitness routine because it provided structure, gave him a feeling of power, and made him physically more imposing, something he found advantageous when using intimidation tactics in the boardroom.

He and Jenny engaged in a few more minutes of small talk, at which point Condon enquired as to her vocation.

"Vacation and travel coordinator," she said, still smiling. "Independent operator. It's perfect. Low stress, and the hours give me plenty of time to write."

A travel agent. All her schooling and all her potential, and she had ended up a travel agent. "You book leisure travel for rich people," he said.

"Yes, and I provide an escape for company employees."

"Escape?" Something in Condon's tone caused Jenny's smile to disappear.

"Yeah, you know, from the grind. These company folks are miserable. Dying to get away."

Condon stared hard at Jenny, unable to mask his disgust

as she finished her drink. "Well, what about you? Are you happy?" she asked.

He remained silent, simply staring at her, utterly dumbfounded. Finally, he said, "What does happy have to do with anything?"

Now it was Jenny's turn to be silent as she searched for something in his eyes. Clearly not finding it, she said, "Sorry, I forgot, cogs in a machine don't get to be happy."

She paid for her drink and left without another word.

The Pack was gathered just beyond scanning range of Staryard Enc-1.

Tarsigh stood on a deck overlooking *Skipjack's* docking bay two. The cruiser *Traveler*, among a handful of other small vessels, sat below. Striker and Findlay were standing nearby in their "sheepskins"—garb that average-income citizens, called sheep, throughout the system would wear—with minimal body armor underneath. The bag slung over one of Striker's shoulders would serve to transport the adaptor back, and Tarsigh knew full well that it currently contained a centrifugal sling gun. One bag was discreet enough; if all three carried them, it might attract attention.

The access door whooshed open and Aladhra stepped through. The beads were gone, and her hair was down, flowing over her shoulders in a fashion that was both exceedingly feminine and markedly out of place for his adopted daughter. Most striking, however, was the simple fact that she wore makeup. He hadn't even known she owned makeup. It lent her features not just enhanced beauty but maturity. The girl he had raised was nowhere to be seen, replaced now by this independent, iron-willed woman.

She had grown up so fast. Too fast. And she had been through more in her short life than anyone should have to go through. As always, there were so many things he wanted to say to her, not the least of which was how beautiful she looked.

Right now she was eyeballing him sternly, no doubt wondering why he was staring at her. Tarsigh realized his mouth was hanging open. He shut it and said, "You should all get going."

Less than a minute later, he was back on the bridge. Braxx stood near the captain's chair, staring off to one side at a monitor mounted to the bulkhead. Findlay's substitute, the rail-thin Jepps, entered and sat at the nav controls.

"Jepps! Welcome to the bridge. Try not to destroy anything," Tarsigh said.

"Aye, cap," Jepps replied.

Tarsigh watched through the observation window as the *Traveler* zoomed off in the direction of the staryard.

Braxx called out for the monitor to increase the volume of an ISNN broadcast, live, though delayed, from Earth's High Court. Dane Koros's trial was about to start.

The judge, a weathered man with a deeply creased face, said, "Let it be known that Dane Koros is hereby charged by the Collective with sedition, a crime punishable by death. Mister Koros, do you understand the charge as I have stated it?"

The camera cut to Koros, his once-dark hair now ghostly white, his eyes sunken above jutting cheekbones. "I do," he answered.

Tarsigh stared at his old friend. He looked terrible.

"And you have elected to represent yourself in these proceedings?" the judge continued.

"I have," Koros answered.

The words "then this trial will now begin" were accompanied by the smashing of a gavel.

From the comm station, Gungan announced that the *Traveler* had passed screening and was on final approach to Staryard Enc-1.

Tarsigh acknowledged the statement when Gungan quickly followed with "Sub-Captain Bloom of the *Harrier* is asking if you received the encrypted message?"

"What encrypted message?" Tarsigh replied.

Braxx called for the monitor to mute.

"Checking," Gungan said. Then: "A message came through the secure channel. A bounty is being offered for the kill or capture of all Pack members and delivery of Pack vessels to the Collective."

"A bounty?" Jepps blurted. "How much?"

"One billion chits," Gungan answered.

"One billion chits," Tarsigh repeated, barely above a whisper.

His guts clenched. A host of thoughts flooded his mind: the Collective had put up the bounty. Did they know about the cube? Most likely not. It was the skip tech they were after. But if his team was captured and delivered to the Collective, they would be probed. Not only did Striker know about the skip tech . . . he and the others knew about the cube. Which meant their leverage would be lost. But the most terrifying thought of all was that they would all be tried and executed.

Aladhra would be executed. If she didn't kill herself first, to prevent her knowledge falling into Collective hands. The mere thought of it caused his heart to falter.

He shared a look with Braxx, now pale-faced. "Patch me through to the *Traveler*, immediately."

"You're through," Gungan said.

"*Traveler*, it's Tarsigh. Abort. Word just came through there's a bounty on our heads. We can't risk it."

Aladhra's voice sounded through the speakers: "We've begun docking maneuvers. We'll be in and out. This is worth it."

"One billion chits, Ladhi," Braxx pressed. "Every pirate in the system'll be out for us."

"Abort!" Tarsigh barked. "That's an order."

There was silence for a moment. Aladhra's voice came back a second later: "No. We need the adaptor, and this may be our only chance to get it."

Tarsigh voiced a string of curses at high volume and kicked the captain's seat as Aladhra's voice declared, "We're going in."

Condon sat in the *Spearhead* dining quarters en route back to Earth, downing a last sip of whiskey and wondering why he was still perturbed by Jenny's words.

He was so out of it he didn't even hear Bullock approach. She sat a full glass down next to his empty one, said, "Looks like you could use a refill," and then took a seat not far from him on the circular couch.

A female voice announced over the speakers: "Message for Brenn Condon."

Condon could take the message privately in his quarters if he wished, but if it was what he thought it was, he wanted Bullock to hear it. "Play message," he replied.

"This is Stephenson. Ran that hack you asked for and I'm happy to report it was a success. We've got ears on their channel."

"End message," the automated voice announced.

Bullock was looking at Condon questioningly.

Condon took a slug of the whiskey and said, "I ordered a hack on Redding's system. It worked. We can now listen in on the encrypted channel he uses to communicate to the Ridgerunners."

He had considered having Redding arrested for communications violations (which wouldn't violate the offer for immunity against charges of sedition), but it was better for appearances—at least for now—that Redding retain his position to reinforce the legitimacy of the bounty.

Bullock opened her mouth to speak, but Condon held up a hand and said, "Control: message to MARSA Collective Oversight Offices."

"Proceed," the computer advised.

"By executive order of the Collective, it is hereby commanded that the independent operator's license issued to Jenny Cooper be revoked. End message."

"Acknowledged," the computer answered. There. Perhaps Jenny would learn something from all of this.

Condon set down the glass. His eyelids felt suddenly heavy.

"You went behind my back," Bullock said. "Looks like

we'll have to work on our communication skills."

Before Condon could reply, the world became dark and distant.

CHAPTER 9

The scene upon their approach had been an impressive one, Aladhra had to admit. Passing through one of Saturn's rings, they had come to Staryard Enc-1, an expansive array of maintenance bays stacked around a central core. And nearby, she was granted her first close-up view of the stark-white, fissured exterior of Enceladus. Though other habitable bodies in the system had been terraformed, this moon had been left unaltered, save for the ice mining scars that ran all across its surface.

The *Traveler* soon berthed in the lowest of several visitor bays occupying the yard's bottom levels.

"Striker!" Tarsigh yelled into Aladhra's earpiece. "Findlay!

Make her see some sense and get back here! NOW!"

She removed her earpiece as she prepared to debark. Striker and Findlay had both paused, unsure. Aladhra reached out and snatched the earpiece from Striker.

"Let's go," she said and opened the inner airlock.

She turned back, waiting expectantly. Findlay looked at Striker, shrugged, and removed his earpiece in the midst of Tarsigh's irate commands.

Once the trio had made it onto the station, Striker said, "He's meeting us on the Level Six Concourse."

Aladhra nodded and looked over to Findlay, who had been grinning like a little kid since they had taken their seats in the cruiser.

It was like he never—

And then Aladhra realized: Findlay had been right. He never got to go anywhere. In all the years she had known him, she could count the number of times on one hand that she had seen him leave the ship. Now that she thought about it, she found it rather funny that they had a navigation officer who never went anywhere and a communications officer who hardly ever said anything.

They took a lift to level six and exited. Findlay separated from them, gawking at his surroundings. Aladhra was impressed as well. Though she had been to more places than Findlay, the staryard was more immaculate than most locations she had visited. Every surface was pristine. Fountains gushed. Luxurious couches accommodated customers waiting for ship repairs to be completed, many of them eating and drinking products purchased at the upstairs food court. At the outer boundaries of the cavernous space, floor-to-ceiling windows allowed a 360-degree view showcasing Enceladus, where geysers of water vapor jetted from the south pole into space and, beyond that, Saturn's roiling troposphere.

Aladhra didn't know what Garth looked like, so she waited for Striker, who was scanning the many faces. His head craned to the second floor; a look of acknowledgment transformed his features as he smiled, waved, then motioned for Aladhra to follow him.

She looked up to spot a man with a stylistically groomed beard and protruding gut. "Findlay, let's go!" she called.

Findlay, who had been smelling a potted plant, followed as they proceeded up the nearest stairs.

On the second floor, the two men exchanged greetings and embraced. Striker introduced Aladhra and Findlay. "So, you've brought me a gift?" Striker asked.

Garth removed a pack from his shoulder. "That I have. Not many of these to be found. Europans aren't big fans of cross-compatibility." He chuckled and opened the bag so Striker could look in.

"Uh-huh, good," Striker said.

Running his free hand through his hair, Garth glanced around. Something about his behavior was raising flags for Aladhra. She quickly assessed their surroundings: there were many customers throughout, but coming from the food court was a tall, bald man in brown utility robes, the kind that were cut to allow for freedom of movement. She reoriented her gaze to the stairs, where another bald man in similar robes was ascending. Yet another robed subject was approaching the far staircase.

"Striker," Aladhra interrupted. "Selected." She bit back a host of curses, not just in response to the situation, but aimed at herself. The call for the team to continue despite the bounty had been hers, and it had been the wrong call. She had brought the Selected right to them.

The Selected were a hybrid science/religious cult and band of Ridgerunners who believed in a god that rewarded the strongest and most highly evolved human beings with an eternally blissful afterlife. Their name was a reference to Darwin's theory of natural selection, but many of them possessed traits that were not improved naturally. Due to bio-enhancements, gene therapy, and augmentation, all Selected were bald, and most were slender and taller than average.

Striker and Findlay both looked and realized Aladhra was right.

Striker snatched the pack from Garth and locked his free hand around the other man's throat. "I vouched for you," he hissed. "Said you were solid. That you had a reputation to uphold . . ."

Aladhra grabbed Garth's bag, closed it, and slipped it on while Findlay retrieved his earpiece.

"It's gone bad," Findlay reported. "Selected." He then winced at the string of profanity streaming back in response.

Aladhra replaced her own earpiece in time to hear Tarsigh say, "On our way." Findlay cast his eyes about frantically. Aladhra kept scanning as well. The Selected silently, slowly tightened the noose.

Garth's face had turned a deep shade of red. His eyes and cheeks bulged as he croaked, "With what I—got saved—and my cut I could—disappear forever."

"You wanna disappear?" Striker asked. He forced the shorter man to the railing, grasped Garth's belt, and hefted him up and over. His terrified scream was cut short seconds later when his bulky frame hit the floor.

The Selected on the second floor produced a disc from the front of his robes. He equipped the disc to his right arm, which Aladhra now guessed was a prosthetic. It appeared that he was arming a centrifugal gun—electrically powered and recoilless, just like the sling gun.

"Go, go!" Striker yelled, pushing Aladhra toward the stairs.

Findlay followed and passed Aladhra on the first few steps as she paused to look back at Striker. He had removed the sling gun from his now-discarded pack, but before he could bring it to bear, the Selected raised his hand, palm out. In the center of that palm was a hole. Or more specifically, a barrel.

Striker hunched down, hopping onto the first set of steps. Aladhra backed down and crouched as a hail of gunfire blazed just over their heads. She collided with Findlay, who was looking to the wraparound windows. They cracked beneath the barrage, but the immensely thick pressure-glass stood up to the small-caliber rounds.

"Duck, you two!" Striker commanded.

Findlay and Aladhra stopped and did as they were told. The ascending cultist on the stairs, holding a pressure blade, looked up just in time to register surprise before a near-solid mass of rounds from Striker's sling gun violently aerated the entirety of his upper torso. Striker then swung the weapon over to the far staircase and cut loose a withering torrent of fire on the second robed subject.

Aladhra gained the last few stairs and vaulted over the handrail, followed by Striker and Findlay. The three ran beneath the second floor toward the nearest lift. Customers throughout the concourse were now screaming and running in a blind panic.

In Aladhra's headset, Tarsigh yelled, "Where you docked?"

"Level one, bay five," Findlay quickly responded.

"Get there quick as you can!" the captain commanded.

As the crowd ahead parted, Aladhra now gained a clear view of the lift bank. . . and the five approaching Selected between it and them.

Tarsigh ordered the Pack to move in on Staryard Enc-1.

The Selected were not their only current enemy. Time was now their next greatest threat. Once the Pack ships bypassed the screening stations, an alert would be sent to the nearest outpost, where the local Collective military would immediately scramble a response.

The nearest screening station issued orders that the Pack ignored as they passed Saturn's outer ring and arrived just outside the yard.

"Jepps, maneuver us to level one," Tarsigh ordered from his seat.

"On it," Jepps responded.

Braxx was standing inches from the observation window, as if he might break through it at any second to retrieve their comrades.

Tarsigh had no doubt that his old friend would do exactly that, were it within the realm of possibility. He scratched at the shaved right side of his head. Why would the Selected attack Aladhra and the others while the deal was happening? Why not wait and follow them back? By attacking during the transaction, the Selected may have wagered that the Pack would come to the rescue. But they would *still* be outgunned. Unless . . .

"Braxx," Tarsigh called. The big man strode over. "Scan the yard for hostiles. Shields, armament, everything."

Braxx nodded and ran to Aladhra's station. "Scanning now. Mm. Yeah. Vessel at 20.32. Gamma class. Weapons hot."

"Ready all weapons, code red," Tarsigh commanded as he pulled up a tactical display.

"Aye," Braxx responded.

"Another ship, delta class," Braxx blurted. "Left one of the docking bays, weapons ready—and another, and—I'm tracking seven ships launching from various maintenance bays."

Tarsigh could see on the display multiple red dots emerging from the yard. He cursed through gritted teeth. The Selected had laid a careful trap . . .

And because of Aladhra, he had led the Pack straight into it.

CHAPTER 10

"Gungan, open tactical channel," Tarsigh said.

"Open," Gungan replied.

"All ships, this is Tarsigh," the captain said. "Multiple hostiles inbound from the yard. Divide and engage until we get our people back on board the *Skipjack*. Tarsigh out."

"Two ships closing on our position, beta class," Braxx announced.

Tarsigh looked again to the display and to the approaching dots. "Shields up."

Braxx shifted over to his own station. "Done."

"Jepps, get us just outside bay five," Tarsigh commanded. "And open our docking bay doors."

"Sir."

Trading fire with both Selected ships at once was a losing proposition. For now, he would just have to hope the shields would hold until Aladhra and the others came back in the cruiser, at which point they could drop shields long enough to dock the incoming ship and skip out, back to where Tarsigh had left drones for all six ships in the fleet.

From the corner of his eye, he caught Braxx casting a worried glance over his shoulder. "Come on, Ladhi, come on."

Striker got off three short bursts before getting the sling gun knocked from his grip by a cultist. The force of the blow made Aladhra think the Selected possessed augmented strength. Even as she continued mentally berating herself for getting all of them into this, she wondered what surprises lay in store for her as she confronted the closest foe. The man was lanky, with dark skin and bulging brown eyes. Her question was immediately answered as her opponent executed two strikes in a blur of movement, catching Aladhra in the face and forcing her to slip back and circle to the cultist's nondominant side.

Speed enhancement. Fantastic. At least the one Findlay was going against was wounded.

Even as she considered this, however, she heard a loud pop and saw Findlay fall in her peripheral vision, the "wounded" cultist standing over him with a telescoping bang-staff. If the bald woman had fired a slug at point-blank range, the navigator might very well be dead . . . because of her.

Aladhra moved evasively but not nearly fast enough: as she absorbed another series of lightning-blows, backpedaling frantically, her foot caught something and slipped out from under her. She landed flat on her back, the bag carrying the adaptor punching into her spine and driving the air from her lungs. Her attacker, however, had paused, looking at what Aladhra had slipped on . . .

Striker's gun.

Instinctively she kicked the weapon back over toward Striker. Her opponent watched the gun slide, distracted just long enough for Aladhra to gain her feet and put all of her weight behind a looping roundhouse punch. The strike connected with the bug-eyed man's jaw just as he faced forward again; his head wobbled, and a single tooth flew from his mouth. He dropped to his knees and fell to his back, one knee still bent, out cold.

Striker had apparently thrown a punch that the other man caught, and was about to have his arm broken when he spotted the gun. As Aladhra closed the distance, Striker swept up the weapon and with his good hand fired directly into his opponent's gut. Blood ejected from the other side as the freakishly strong cultist let go of his arm and slumped to the floor.

Striker spun toward Aladhra, shouting, "Down!"

Aladhra crouched and looked over her shoulder; Striker's burst struck the bang-staff-wielding woman, ripping upward from her belly to the top of her head, nearly splitting her in half.

Before she could tend to Findlay, Aladhra had to know that the immediate threat was neutralized. She scanned the room, and sure enough, over at the stairs she spotted the cultist with the prosthetic arm hopping over the handrail and landing nimbly.

"Stairs!" she shouted to Striker, who sprayed a barrage of fire that succeeded in cutting the man down. More were coming, though, surely . . .

"Outside," she heard Striker say.

She looked beyond the stairs, through the observation window, to see the Pack ship *Harrier* squaring off against a Selected craft. *Harrier* had her shields up and the Selected vessel was firing; the rounds deflecting from the shield were coming dangerously close . . .

She rushed to her fallen comrade and dragged him to an open lift as plasma rounds tore through the wraparound windows, opening the concourse to the vacuum of space.

Striker lunged for the lift and barely made it inside behind her. The doors closed as the few customers who hadn't fled were swept up and out, along with plants and the bodies of fallen cultists. Aladhra punched a button, and the lift descended. They watched through the transparent shell as the car sank below the upper floor to where fountain water was streaming towards the pressure breach. Finally, the lift passed below the floor, and as they proceeded down, they were able to shift attention to Findlay.

Most of his left forearm was simply gone, the hand being attached only by strands of muscles and tendon. A significant chunk of his right forearm was missing as well, the bones splintered. His eyes were rolling up and his body was a limp mass on the floor.

Setting aside the empty bag, Striker ripped fabric from his shirt to use as tourniquets and applied them to each arm.

"We just need to keep him from bleeding out," he said to Aladhra, sweat dripping from his forehead.

She handed back the earpiece she had taken from him as the lift at last reached level one.

Striker lifted Findlay under the armpits and dragged him out into the main reception area. Aladhra had taken the sling gun, which she now aimed at the security personnel who waited near the visitor's bay access. A woman behind the long reception desk in the corner squealed as Aladhra yelled, "Drop your guns!" The two yard guards complied, lifting their hands in the air. Striker laid Findlay down and gathered the guns while Aladhra turned and blasted the controls for all three lifts in the bank.

A window on the wall adjacent to the visitor access allowed a view of the action taking place just outside. Aladhra glanced there long enough to see *Skipjack's* shields deflecting massive volumes of firepower from not one, but two Selected vessels.

"*Skipjack's* shields won't hold," she said to Striker, who was watching as well.

"No, and we can't get back until she drops her shields . . ."

"And when she does those ships will rip her to pieces."

Striker was nodding. "Get Findlay to the *Traveler* and make ready to launch when I say," he declared as he made a beeline for the staircase.

"We're not leaving without you!" she yelled after him.

"I'll join you, don't worry. Just go. Now!" Striker rushed up the steps.

———•———

"**S**hield strength at forty percent," Braxx reported.

Tarsigh had moved directly to the observation window, looking out at the staryard. He ran one scenario after another through his mind; each ended with their bloody ruin.

He ordered Gungan to open the tactical channel and said, "All ships, report status."

The *Harrier*, *Death Rattle*, *Talon*, *Monolith*, and *Rapier* all reported varying amounts of damage or shield degradation. The Pack ships reporting damage had opted to forego shields and go head-to-head against their attackers. The captain had hoped that maybe one of them could overcome their adversary and then come to aid the *Skipjack*, but the Pack and Selected vessels, it seemed, were too evenly matched.

Their options were diminishing by the second.

"We have to get them on board," Braxx called.

"I know," Tarsigh responded.

"The shields won't hold! And when they're gone—"

"I know!" he yelled back, spit flying. "Don't you think I know that?"

Just then, Striker's voice came through the speakers: "Captain, need you to hang on just a little longer. Make ready to lower shields and receive the *Traveler* on my signal."

What signal? he wondered. But if Striker had wanted to share that information, he would have.

"Copy," Tarsigh replied. Whatever it was Striker had in mind, the captain just hoped it would be enough.

———•———

Striker's thoughts raced. He felt like a complete ramrod. The meeting had been *his* idea. The traitorous slug Garth had been *his* recommendation. If it hadn't been for him, Findlay wouldn't be barely clinging to life right now. Whatever it took, he had to set this right. He did have an idea. It was reckless, to say the least . . . but reckless was what he did best. Not to mention that it might also be the only chance they had.

He burst into the control room for maintenance bay A-4, the bay located above level one.

"Release the docking clamps, chubby," he ordered the controller, gun aimed at the large man's head.

The wide-eyed employee complied. Striker fired a burst into the controls and told the man to flee, which he did without hesitation.

The maintenance bays were all partially enclosed by a roof and two walls. Mounted to the side-shells were docking clamps, a safety feature to hold the vessels in place while maintenance progressed. Striker peered out the gallery window to the docked ship, where tethered engineers in pressure suits appeared to be repairing a port-side thruster. It was a mid-sized ice hauler. No armament, but that wouldn't matter.

Time to separate the men from the boys.

Striker bolted into the corridor. Seconds later he was at the airlock, then through and into the ship.

He mused that Findlay's navigational expertise would have come in handy at this moment as he sprinted through the vessel to the bridge.

Nevertheless, Striker knew enough. He would make

this work. Through the observation window, a few hundred meters away, one of the Selected vessels fired down onto the *Skipjack*.

"Whatever you're doing, I suggest doing it now," Tarsigh's strained voice announced in Striker's earpiece.

Striker fired up the ship's engines, set the thrusters for maximum launch speed, and set a timer for activation. He then ran for the vessel's only lifepod.

Aladhra was out of breath as she sat at the *Traveler's* controls, having hauled Findlay's not-exactly-light frame through the visitor area to the berth where they had docked.

Findlay lay on the floor behind her, unresponsive.

It was all her fault.

She had insisted, even after Tarsigh had warned them. And now, Findlay was on the verge of dying because of her bullheadedness. But there was no time to dwell on it. Findlay would live. And Striker would come through, as he always did.

As if in response to her thoughts, Striker's voice sounded over the tactical channel: "*Traveler*, launch. *Skipjack*, drop shields on my mark and focus all firepower on the vessel to your starboard side."

"Copy," Tarsigh confirmed.

"Aye," Aladhra replied.

———◆———

Tarsigh stroked his chin, attention fixed on the tactical display.

"Shields at 15 percent," Braxx announced.

"Jepps," Tarsigh said, "confirm velocity match on all drones."

"Sir. All drones are matching Pack velocities."

"Gravity?"

"Adjusted."

"Good. Gungan, tactical."

"Done."

"All ships, make ready to skip on my command," Tarsigh informed. A second later he was relieved to hear Aladhra's voice. "*Traveler* en route," she said.

"10 percent," Braxx reported.

"*Skipjack*, mark," Striker cut in.

"Missile and starboard battery lock confirm," Tarsigh ordered.

"Confirmed," Braxx replied. "Shields at 5—"

"Lower shields," Tarsigh commanded.

"Lowered," Braxx replied as the ship rocked in response to incoming plasma rounds.

"Fire!" Tarsigh ordered.

Striker had to time it just perfectly. Launch too early and he would blast himself right into the maintenance bay shell; too late and he would be obliterated along with the ship. He sat in the lifepod, taking deep breaths, waiting for the countdown to hit zero. It did. The transport's drive kicked in. The vessel blasted from the bay; Striker launched the pod . . .

And let loose with a victorious howl the instant he realized that he had timed it just right. Through the ship's porthole, he glimpsed the hauler ramming at full speed into the Selected ship that had taken position above the *Skipjack*. The collision resulted in a spectacular dissolution of both vessels. He didn't have eyes on the *Skipjack* yet, but if Tarsigh had done as asked, all of the *Skipjack's* significant armament should now be directed at the second Selected ship, the one that had been situated at *Skipjack's* starboard side.

The *Skipjack* took several hits, including a buster-seeker missile combo, the same tactic they had used on the Collective ship *Imperious*. Not only were their shields nonfunctional, tactical scanners and displays were disabled as well.

As a result, Tarsigh was relying on good old-fashioned eyesight, standing with a very anxious Braxx at the observation window and watching the *Traveler* make her approach.

Even with tactical out, Tarsigh could see that Striker had managed to launch a vessel from the yard into the *Skipjack's* second Selected attacker—a gutsy gambit that Tarsigh would most definitely have to congratulate his tech officer on. Assuming Striker would make it back on board.

Thankfully, the tactic had worked: the *Skipjack* had weathered the storm from their remaining adversary and launched an all-out attack of their own that crippled the vessel.

"Message coming through on the open channel," Gungan announced.

"Put it through," Tarsigh said.

"Pirate vessels of the Pack, this is Captain Albright of the Collective ship *Peerless*. You are surrounded."

Tarsigh could no longer see the *Traveler*, but Aladhra's voice came through a second after the *Peerless* captain's. "We're on board," she said.

"YES!" Braxx yelled at Tarsigh's side, causing him to jump. He sighed in relief. But where was Striker?

The *Peerless* commander's voice came back through the speakers: "Pack flagship—whatever designation you choose—you are hereby ordered to surrender all vessels."

They wanted the tech. The Collective wouldn't blow them to pieces because of the Europan tech integrated in the Pack ships.

Just then he thought he saw a lifepod zoom past the window.

"Pack flagship, prepare to be boarded," the *Peerless* captain said.

"I'm here," Striker's voice announced. "Go go go!"

Tarsigh smiled, slapping Braxx on the back. "Gungan, tactical," he said.

"Done."

"All ships, skip on my mark . . ."

The floor trembled slightly. That would be the *Peerless's* umbilical attaching to their port-side airlock. A heavily armed boarding team would be storming through the passage, prepared to cut their way in . . .

A shame they would be greeted with empty space.

"Mark," Tarsigh said.

CHAPTER 11

Condon awoke in his cabin as the *Spearhead* broke Earth's atmosphere.

His head pounded; it felt as if his brain were pushing against the inside of his skull. As he made the effort to sit up, he detected another pain, this one a stinging sensation in the back of his neck. His probing fingers discovered a bump there, sensitive to touch. It wasn't raised, like a bug bite. It was more like the sore spot caused by . . . an injection. He sprang up, steadied himself in reaction to dizziness, and proceeded to the washroom, staring in the mirror, taking deep breaths. He told himself to calm down. Think.

He struggled to access his last memory. His thoughts

were jumbled, muddy. He had spoken to Jenny . . . at the bar. And then, he had come back on board the ship, to return to Earth. He had been drinking; he had arranged for Jenny to lose her license . . .

Pain, like a tightening fist, caused him to grasp at his head. He took slower breaths and fought through. Once the pain-wave subsided, he continued his attempts at recollection.

Bullock. Bullock had been there. She had given him a drink.

Seconds later he was moving carefully through the *Spearhead* corridor and then he stood in front of Bullock's door, hammering on it.

Bullock opened it, eyebrows tightly knitted, obviously perturbed at the intrusion.

"What did you do to me?" he demanded.

"Come again?"

"You put something in my drink, and while I was out you messed with my head. I want to know exactly what you did."

He had taken a step forward, just an inch from Bullock, who stared up with a hard, steady gaze.

"I didn't 'do' anything. You consumed a fair amount of alcohol, and you started behaving in an unprofessional manner."

"You're lying!" Condon blurted, leaning so that he was nearly nose to nose with Bullock, who stayed still as a statue.

Just then, a light vibrating sensation in both Condon and Bullock's arms informed them that a message was awaiting their attention.

Bullock pivoted and strode back into her cabin. She

activated the holo-projector on a table in the sitting area and turned to give Condon an impassive stare.

"You coming in?"

Condon hesitated only briefly before stepping into the room. He was still fixing Bullock with a stern gaze as an automated voice informed her that the message was forwarded by the Collective Lead Operations Manager, Enceladus. Bullock then played the message. A holographic head appeared on the table, displaying the features of a nervous-looking Collective military captain.

"I am Captain Albright of the Collective Frigate *Peerless*, filing my report of an encounter with the group of Ridgerunners known as the Pack."

Albright went on to explain how his armada had been on training maneuvers when the call had come in that a bloody conflict between two suspected pirate groups had erupted on board Staryard Enc-1. He went on to report that by the time his armada had arrived, the confrontation had expanded to include several ships on both sides, just outside the yard.

"We established a perimeter, and I felt that, given the amount of damage the two groups had inflicted on each other, we had the situation well in hand. The Pack, however . . ." Albright hesitated here. "The Pack vanished before we could board their flagship. We nearly lost three men, but they were in pressure suits and we were able to retrieve them."

Condon knew that Collective military throughout the system had been informed to be on the lookout for the Pack and not to destroy the ships when encountered but to board and take possession. As far as Condon knew, the military had not been fully briefed on the new technology the Pack possessed.

"Six drones appeared . . . it seems they took the place of the Pack vessels. All six of the drones have been collected and brought on board the *Peerless*. The second Ridgerunner element, known as the Selected, have been taken into custody along with their ships. I will hold them until I receive further orders. This is Captain Albright, concluding my report."

Condon cursed, shaking his head. "He had them. Had them and he let them go. Idiot! At least he got the drones."

It would be up to the Old Man as to whether that would be enough to spare Captain Albright from the grisly fate that awaited all who failed the Collective.

Bullock, for some reason, was looking at Condon and smiling. Condon frowned at the woman. "What the hell are you smiling about?"

"It's working. The plan is working. The Selected failed, but it just goes to show that the Ridgerunners are willing to turn on their own for the right price. The Pack escaped, but now there will be nowhere for them to hide. Tell me . . . what are your thoughts on how to handle the Selected?"

The heat that had been boiling within Condon had now subsided somewhat. "Much as I hate to admit it, I think we should process them and then let them go. It won't do much to demonstrate the validity of our bounty if we arrest and try the pirates who attempt to collect it."

"Agreed," Bullock said flatly. "I'll run it past the Old Man." She continued staring at Condon, who simply gazed back. "About the other matter: I suggest you abandon any misguided notions of wrongdoing on my part. We can put all of that nonsense behind us and we can continue working together. Or . . . I can take this to HR."

Her unblinking eyes held him. Condon weighed his

options carefully. Her word against his. But maybe that was what she wanted. What exactly was she playing at? Clearly, she was pursuing her own agenda. She was aware that the Old Man was grooming his replacement, and whatever she had done was an effort to sabotage him and elevate herself in his eyes. By losing his patience, coming here, accusing her, he had played into her hands . . .

With a forced smile, Condon said, "Consider the matter forgotten," then turned and walked away.

The pilot announced their final approach as Condon entered his cabin, rubbing the back of his head. The pain there was related to whatever power play she was conducting. She had most definitely done *something* to him. For now, though, he would play her game. Meanwhile . . .

He would use his own methods to find out exactly what she was attempting and put a very definitive end to it.

"You hashed it!" Tarsigh yelled.

Aladhra bit back a response. Barely.

Veins stood out on the captain's neck where the cobra slithered away to be replaced by the dragon. "You don't want me telling you what to do, I get that. But guess what, I'm the captain! You're not! I don't care if you don't like that, because your refusal to obey orders nearly got all of us killed!"

It was just the two of them in the *Skipjack* meeting room. Aladhra remained silent, leaning back in her chair, staring at nothing in particular. He was right. And she *hated* when he was right.

Following an initial test, Striker had reported that the adaptor taken from Garth did in fact work. And Findlay—Findlay would live. The ship's med tech, Fowler, had stopped the bleeding immediately when Aladhra brought the dying man aboard. But there was no denying that her fellow Pack member had nearly died. Or that he was in danger of losing at least one arm. *Or* that the entire Pack had been at risk of getting captured or, yes, killed.

And the fault lay squarely on her shoulders.

"I wonder if this hate you have for me could be set aside," Tarsigh said in a much lower tone, the crimson fading from his skin as he leaned on the table with both hands. "At least until the immediate danger has passed. Then . . . then you can hate me all you want, how's that?"

Aladhra rose from her chair and walked to the observation window. "I don't hate you," she said quietly, looking out to where a scattered confusion of metal pieces floated against a smattering of stars.

Following the encounter at Staryard Enc-1, the Pack had limped its way to a Ridge scrap field—one of many dumping grounds for junk; everything from obsolete drives to entire shells of vessels of all types and sizes had been brought to this boneyard and abandoned. Hundreds of meters of discarded, forgotten trash. Machinery and components that had once meant something to someone.

Aladhra realized she was grinding her teeth. "I don't hate you, but I also don't need you to rub my nose in it," she said.

"I'm not trying to—" Tarsigh began, but he was cut off when Braxx's voice broke in over the room's comm.

"Cap, you wanted an update on repairs."

With a long exhale, Tarsigh hit the comm button and sat. "Yeah, where are we?"

"Level three hull breach is our biggest concern," Braxx announced. "I've got grappling drones outside, collecting and cutting scrap. The patch job'll take time. Two rotations is my guess."

Aladhra turned from the window. Tarsigh looked as if he were ready to punch something. Instead, he replied, "Okay. Copy that."

Tarsigh didn't look her way, but he didn't have to. Suddenly the conference room felt entirely too small. She needed to be somewhere else. "I'll check on Findlay," she said and left the room.

Tarsigh remained in the conference room, listening as the sub-captains gave their updates one by one over the comm: *Talon* and *Monolith* had maintained shields throughout the engagement and had taken no damage. *Harrier*, *Death Rattle*, and *Rapier*, however, were in bad shape. Each of them would need one to two rotations to complete their own repair work.

Tarsigh acknowledged their reports and then sat, alone with his thoughts. He knew that Aladhra was her own harshest critic. What had happened to Findlay would eat at her. But she needed to understand that decisions carried consequences. It was a tough lesson, and one he himself knew all too well.

He left the conference room, making his way distractedly

to meet with Striker, all the time wondering if he had been too harsh with her. Or was he not harsh enough? Had he been too soft on her all of these years? Or did she need her space? And did those needs change over time, from childhood to adulthood? Someone should write a manual on such things. As he approached the ship's largest processing room, he set his doubts aside and turned his thoughts once again to the matters at hand.

Striker acknowledged him with a dip of the chin as Tarsigh entered. The cube was there in the center of the floor, while a floating holographic screen displayed the data streaming onto the ship's servers.

Striker punched a few buttons on a datapad in his left hand and said, "The amount of dirt the Europans stockpiled against the Collective is unbelievable," he said. "It stretches back over a hundred spans."

"So why aren't you smiling?"

"No, really, this is everything we hoped for. It's just . . . Garth, the staryard, that was my doing . . ."

Tarsigh had no immediate answer. He had been so focused on Aladhra, on her mistake . . . but Striker's situation wasn't the same.

"Let's just say you're a lousy judge of character and leave it at that," the captain said.

Striker exhaled, his tense posture softening.

"I'll let you make up for it . . ." Tarsigh continued. "How many drones are we down to?"

"Ten of the 'specials,' fifteen regular skip-drones."

There was an idea Tarsigh had been mulling over since they had arrived at the scrap field. "There's the issue of the drones left behind at Enceladus. The skip tech can be used to swap drone for drone, not just drone for vessel, correct?"

Striker curled his lower lip, shoulders shrugging slightly. "Same tech, yeah. You want to use a 'special' drone again?"

"I want to go even better than that," Tarsigh replied.

Doc Fowler was in the midst of singing some Martian ballad, scrubbing his hands and arms with disinfectant gel when Aladhra stepped into the med bay. He stopped crooning long enough to say, "Ah, hey, I just finished up. Findlay's awake if you want to see him." He then went back to warbling his love song as Aladhra entered the recovery room.

A wall monitor was displaying rotation two of the Dane Koros trial.

"Do you acknowledge that you acted against the Collective in the Inter-Worlds War?" the Collective prosecutor asked.

"I do," Koros responded, his face filling the monitor.

"So you freely admit to your guilt?" the prosecutor pressed.

"The only thing I'm guilty of," Koros answered, "is battling corruption and tyranny."

Findlay was lying on the bed, his left arm in a rapid-mend cast. His right arm was missing, capped just below the elbow. Aladhra's hands flew to her mouth as she approached, staring at the void where Findlay's arm should be.

"Ladhra! I was hoping I'd get a chance to thank you—" he began before Aladhra cut him off.

"Thank me?" She came to the bedside and laid a hand

on his shoulder.

"Thank you, yeah. You did save my life, and all."

Aladhra hated tears more than just about anything. But there was nothing for it now. Her eyes overflowed. "You lost your arm!" she cried.

"Well, yeah, but doc's gonna fit me with a nifty new prosthetic. Mostly new, anyway. He said it might have a few kinks needin' worked out, but that's—"

Aladhra put a hand to Findlay's mouth and said, "Stop! I'm sorry. Okay? I just came to say I'm sorry."

She spun around and was rushing out of the room as Findlay called after her, "No, it's okay! Don't—"

But Aladhra was already gone, feet pounding a path toward the lift at the end of the corridor, wishing for some kind of pressure release for the emotions that warred within her. On her left, the corridor opened into a gathering room. Everyone on this level was apparently busy; no one was seated in the viewing area, but on the massive wall monitor, the trial continued. Aladhra stopped and stepped into the empty space.

On the monitor, the prosecutor approached the stand. "Do you accept responsibility for your actions as a rebel leader?" he asked.

"My only responsibility was and is to the people, to prove to them that they're more than just cogs in your machine. To inform them that a better life awaits anyone who's willing to fight for it."

"Willing to kill for it, you mean," the prosecutor said. "As you did. Time and again. Apparently without regret."

"I have plenty of regrets," Koros answered. "Foremost among them being that the people of this system have no idea what it is to be truly free. Yes, I have regrets. That's part of what it means to be a leader, to take on responsibility. All too often responsibility and regret go hand in hand. But a true leader learns from their mistakes, so they might prevent others from making those very same ones."

Aladhra's mouth twisted. She nodded her head, wiped at her eyes, then turned and left the room.

CHAPTER 12

Strategic Planning and Advanced Initiatives. That was Bullock's department, and Condon wanted to know exactly what that meant.

For the past day since his return to Earth, he had been debating just how to go about acquiring such information. And then he'd remembered his trip to the moon just less than a cycle ago.

He looked over to a shelf on his wall, where a robotic upper head and torso sat. During Condon's brief stay on the moon he'd used the sit-in android: it was a very simple mechanical bust, designed to look human, that occupied a seat during important meetings while an executive was away. The executive could wear VR goggles that allowed him or her to rotate the head while seeing through the android's eyes, and the executive's voice would issue from the android's mouth. It was the next evolution of video teleconferencing, nearly as good as being physically present. In fact, some departments fabricated face masks for sit-in androids to resemble their true-life counterparts.

One of the departments Condon oversaw was the one responsible for developing and maintaining the sit-in androids.

It was a perfect alignment that had provided an epiphany for Condon. He sat now in his office, a holographic display of the company directory on his canted desktop. He typed in a name: KAMURA, JEFF. Jeff was a team lead in Strategic Planning and Advanced Initiatives. Condon had thought about going after Bullock's android, but given their recent butting of heads, he believed she might be on guard.

Next, Condon pulled up the number for the Android Team Lead, Monte Hutchins, and hit the call button. Monte answered on the first ring.

"Hutchins. Condon here. I want you to bring in Jeff Kamura's sit-in android for routine maintenance."

"Jeff . . ."

"Kamura. Strategic Planning and Advanced Initiatives."

There was a brief pause while Hutchins most likely tried to puzzle out why such a request was coming seemingly out of the blue. Like a good company man, however, Hutchins answered "right away" a second later.

"Good," Condon replied. "Let me know as soon as it's in. I'll want to have a talk with the engineer. Put Teller on it."

"Teller, yes sir," Hutchins said.

Condon ended the call. The wheels were in motion. He would have to be careful, be ready to cover his steps. Obfuscate. But gathering this intelligence was critical in planning next steps. For if Condon was right, Bullock had established herself as his enemy.

And enemies must always be crushed, swiftly and completely.

The message had come through late in the night while Condon had been sleeping. The Collective ship *Peerless* had suffered a catastrophe when her entire cargo hold had been obliterated in some kind of explosion, killing Captain Albright and four engineers.

At this time, no one knew exactly what had happened. Condon had a guess—it stood to reason that the drones could trade places with something that could be rigged to detonate—but that speculation was certainly not an opinion he would voice until more facts came in. If Condon's suspicions proved correct, it might be yet one more thing he could leverage against Bullock, by saying that the idea to transport the drones without precautions had been hers, and that she had acted alone. The fact that she had been the one to give the order for transport certainly worked in Condon's favor.

He had exited the shuttlecar and made his way into lab six on the Collective Headquarters campus. Once past all of the security screenings, he made his way to the primary maintenance facility where a bustling workforce went about repairing and servicing various robots and androids. Stanley Teller stood at a workstation with what Condon assumed was Jeff Kamura's sit-in android.

With that assumption confirmed, Condon informed Teller that the two of them should go someplace more private. Inside a meeting room overlooking the main floor minutes later, Condon said, "I'm going to order you to do something shifty, and you're going to do it."

Teller stared back, mouth slightly open, and waited for the executive to continue.

"It came to my attention nearly a full span ago that you had an uncle who fought in the Inter-Worlds War. On the wrong side."

The blood drained from Teller's face as Condon held up a hand. "Honestly I don't care. The actions of your uncle certainly don't make *you* a traitor, do they?"

"Well, no, not at all—I've always been a loyal—"

"I know, that's why I didn't go anywhere with the knowledge. But you can see how that information could be damaging, were it to get out. It could certainly be twisted."

"Why are you—"

"Because I'm trying to catch someone who may actually *be* a traitor. And I need your help. But it must be done discreetly."

A light buzz in Condon's right wrist notified him of a message. He held up a finger to notify Teller to wait, then tapped his arm. The message in his earpiece informed him that the Old Man wanted to see him. Now.

Could he know what Condon was up to somehow? Or was this about the *Peerless*?

One thing Condon had learned was not to let paranoia get the better of him. A bit of paranoia was healthy, but too much could lead one to actions that would greatly exacerbate a situation that might otherwise be managed.

Condon returned his attention to Teller. "Okay, I have to go, but first, this is exactly what I need you to do . . ."

CHAPTER 13

Bullock was already sitting at the Old Man's desk when Condon stepped into his orbiting office, which was currently flying over Saudi Arabia. During the shuttlecar ride, Condon had been on a call with the prosecutor in the Dane Koros trial. It was a seemingly small thing, what Condon had proposed to the lawyer, but one never knew which sparks of inspiration might ignite into all-out flame.

As Condon continued toward the desk he could hear Folk in the en suite washroom, retching. Bullock eyed Condon inscrutably as he sat. They both waited until running water sounded. Folk shuffled out soon after, appearing much more haggard than when Condon had last seen him.

"So you heard about the *Peerless*," the CEO began.

"Yes sir," Bullock said. "I look forward to finding out what happened."

Condon remained silent.

"The investigation's in full swing, but that's not why I called you here. You're here because I'm told that one particular Ridgerunner has information on the whereabouts of the Pack. But he'd only—" Folk paused to cough. "He'd only relay the intelligence to me personally. He's being brought—"

A beeping noise from the Old Man's desk was followed by a secretary announcing that Folk's "visitor" had arrived.

The man who entered a moment later was escorted by three armed guards. He was skinny, with slick, shoulder-length black hair on three-quarters of his head. The hair on a good portion of the left side of his skull was missing. Not shaved, just gone. Burned away, Condon imagined, judging by the scarring that marred the entire left side of the man's face, from forehead to neck, where it conceivably carried on beneath the man's shirt.

Skin covered most of the man's left eye, but the right eye remained steadily fixed on Folk as the guards brought the skinny man to the center of the open space. "Spirion Bak," the man announced.

"What's the information you have and what do you want in return?" the Old Man urged without preamble.

"Oh, the information's plenty," Spirion said. "I know things, see, things you'd prefer the general populace didn't know."

"Nonsense," Folk answered.

Condon had turned in his seat and was listening intently.

Bullock was looking over, hand supporting her chin, eyes narrow.

"You'll wish it was, word gets out. For instance, I know that you introduced the Black Pox on Enceladus so you could make billions off the vaccine."

To his credit, the Old Man kept his poker face. Condon was visibly affected. It was known only at the highest levels that the Collective had both propagated the disease *and* manufactured its cure.

"I can even tell you what ship delivered the pox to Enceladus. The *Steadfast*. Still not impressed? How 'bout this: I can name your entire supply and distribution network for Slipstream. And that's just for—"

Folk held up a hand to silence him. "What do you want?" he asked.

"Why, I want the one billion chits all to myself, o' course."

"And what are you offering?"

"First off, I'm the only person who knows anything about how the Pack's borrowed Europan technology works. You got a line on that, right? I'm guessing they've used it on you, and that's why you want their ships intact."

Folk remained silent. Condon was taken aback. How was it possible that this . . . *nobody* knew so much? It was disturbing, to say the least.

"I'll take that as a 'yes.' So, second thing I'm offerin' is this . . ." Spirion stepped away from the guards, who moved forward with him.

Folk simply waited.

"I know where they're goin' next," Spirion said with a wide grin.

RIDGERUNNERS

———◆———

Aladhra hadn't left her cabin for two full rotations.

She lay in her bunk, staring at the ceiling, half-listening to the time-delayed Dane Koros trial that played on the bulkhead monitor.

The prosecutor asked, "Do you admit to serving in the so-called Death Dealer squad, alongside Cole Darck, August Braxx, Castigan Tarsigh, Valencia—"

"I will not name names," Koros replied.

"Your service as well as the names of those you served with is well documented," the prosecutor replied, but Aladhra was no longer listening.

Ever since the confrontation at Staryard Enc-1, her mind had been a boiling cauldron, one that had only begun to simmer in the past several hours. Over the course of that time, she had thought long and hard about the girl she had been, the woman she had become, and the woman she wanted to be.

She was used to being angry, bitter, frustrated. For most of her life, Tarsigh had borne the brunt of her enmity, for a great many reasons.

But now, after what had happened at Enceladus . . . she was forced to face certain uncomfortable truths. Mainly that she had been unfair. Unreasonable. So consumed and blinded by rage that her judgment had been eclipsed.

Aladhra got up, went into the washroom, and appraised her reflection.

She thought again of Findlay, lying there, missing a piece of himself that he would never get back . . . because of the woman staring back at her.

It took an extreme force of will not to punch the mirror as hard as she could.

Tarsigh took his seat at the head of the table. Braxx sat to his left. The seat to his right, Aladhra's seat, was empty. She had requested time alone and Tarsigh aimed to give it to her; he could always update her afterward. Striker was present, as were Gungan and Findlay, with his new prosthetic arm.

The remaining seats were filled by the Pack sub-captains.

Tarsigh had, at this point, reviewed a good amount of what was on the cube. The revelations offered by that device were illuminating, horrifying, infuriating, and galvanizing.

Striker leaned back in his chair and put his feet on the table, close to Findlay, who shoved them away. Striker belted Findlay on the shoulder, and Findlay answered with a punch from his prosthetic arm, knocking Striker clear out of his seat. The other man came up grimacing, rubbing his shoulder.

"Enough!" Tarsigh said.

Findlay smiled, shaking his new fist in victory before turning his attention to the captain.

"I've called you all here because we have something of immense value in the form of the information stored on the data cube I've told you about. Information that has the power to sway public opinion *against* the Collective. The question I put to you is how to use it."

For a moment there was silence.

Then: "Information of this kind only has two uses," Gordo, sub-captain of the *Monolith*, offered. "As leverage, or as a wake-up call to the masses." His diminutive size meant that he sat lower than everyone else. Though his seat was certainly capable of being raised, it was an option Gordo never exercised.

"Agreed," Tarsigh replied.

"The only way I could see it used as leverage is if we told the Collective to fold up and dissolve all operations, hand over their weapons, surrender . . ." Kring, sub-captain of the *Rapier*, offered. The mocha-skinned Titanian was a heavily-muscled, domineering presence.

"I don't see them doing that," Bard put in. He was sub-captain of the *Talon* and a pirate who had seen more spans than just about any other Pack member. He sat hunched under the weight of his age, his stringy, dirty gray hair hanging like a shroud.

"Neither do I," Tarsigh said.

"Collective's got nothing else I want," Kring concluded.

"We could bargain for the release of Koros," Braxx offered.

"I thought of that as well," Tarsigh replied. "Koros went his own way after the war, but I still understand him well enough to know that he would see us using the information to save him as a gross misuse of something so powerful and so potentially damaging to our greatest enemy."

Braxx sighed, nodding in concession.

"So we wield this information as a weapon," Sub-Captain Auric, of the *Death Rattle*, stated. He was a rangy man, renowned for an *Imperious* demeanor and expensive tastes.

"The question then is how to disseminate it to the people," Tarsigh said.

"There can be no half measures," Gordo replied. "When we pull that trigger, it's all or nothing."

Murmurs of consent echoed throughout the room.

"I think there's only one way," Striker said. "The captain and I have discussed this. We use the only network that's already in place, capable of reaching every colony and outpost in the system: the Inter-Solar News Network."

There were nods of assent all around the table . . . except for Bloom, who seemed lost in his own little world. Bloom was sub-captain of the *Harrier*. Tall and swarthy, he was normally boisterous and the loudest voice in any room, but throughout the meeting he had sat with his head down, drumming his fingers nervously on the table top.

"I see and hear a lot of agreement around the table. Sub-Captain Bloom, what do you think?"

Bloom looked up and over as if he'd just awoken from a fitful sleep. His eyes darted around the table. "Yeah. If everyone's on board then . . . yeah."

Tarsigh's eyes narrowed at the sub-captain's uncharacteristic behavior.

"Network headquarters orbits Mars. Security's tight," Striker said, "but getting there, uploading even just a fraction of what we've got, and broadcasting it . . . it's not impossible. As long as they don't know we're coming."

Tarsigh said, "I've told one of our shipping contacts that we may be sending him some cargo. He's got a vessel hauling supplies out to Farpost Seven." The captain looked to Striker. "When?"

Striker glanced at a time readout on the wall. "Two

hours."

Gordo spoke up: "So the hauler takes six drones to Mars and lets them loose outside the station? Will the drones take up and maintain the proper position?"

"If I program them with the coordinates, yes," Striker answered.

"I'll only make the call if we're all in agreement," Tarsigh put in. He witnessed a table full of nodding heads in return.

He inclined his own to Striker and said, "Okay. Program the drones and get 'em underway."

CHAPTER 14

Aladhra had gotten fully dressed and was set to leave her cabin when the prosecutor's voice caught her ear:

"The Collective will now demonstrate that Dane Koros is a traitor not only to his government—"

"You were never my government," Koros spat.

"But to his own allies," the lawyer concluded. "When you were captured, we recovered comm logs on your ship, the *Redoubt*, dating back to the Inter-Worlds War. Let's take a journey, why don't we . . . back to that time period, twelve spans ago, when you and your Death Dealers waged war on your benefactors."

"You make me sick," Koros said. "Whatever it is you think to prove—"

"The *Vigilant*, a command and control sentry outpost orbiting Mars . . ."

Aladhra stepped over, standing in front of the monitor, riveted.

"It was there that one of the final, most feverish battles took place. You were losing, desperate, so you planted explosives, enough to obliterate the entire station. But you needed someone to buy you time, while you made your escape. So one of your lieutenants, Castigan Tarsigh, tricked another high-ranking officer—and his supposed friend—Cole Darek, to 'hold off' the opposition . . ."

"That's a lie and you know it," Koros shot back, looking as if he might jump over the witness box.

"You knew full well what was happening," the prosecutor said. Then to the camera, he continued, "I present to you exhibit D from the *Redoubt's* own comm logs." He turned to look off camera. "Play it."

"Cowards!" the voice said, and Aladhra's hands flew to her mouth. That was the voice of her father, a voice she had thought never to hear again. "At least finish what you started! You want something to die for? Come back here and I'll give you something to die for, you sons of—"

"That's enough," the prosecutor held up a hand and the recording stopped. "Those don't sound like the words of someone who volunteered to stay behind," he said to Koros.

An ember burned within Aladhra, one that quickly burst into flame that spread through every vein in her body.

"You and Castigan Tarsigh set up your own comrade and left him to die," the prosecutor concluded.

Aladhra saw nothing else, thought nothing else, as she blazed out of the room.

"Aladhra, good, we can catch you up on—" Tarsigh began but then stopped as he registered the blind fury on her face and the cold detachment in her eyes. He frowned; everyone else at the table was silent as Aladhra cut a path straight for the captain and locked both hands on his throat, continuing her momentum and dragging him from his seat.

Still grasping him by the neck, she drove him to the floor, shouting, "You said he 'bought time.' That he died a hero!"

Tarsigh's mind raced: what had she found out? What had she been told? He grasped at the wrists pinning him to the floor, unable to speak, cheeks bulging, fighting for air.

"Ladhi," Braxx said, nearing her.

"BACK!" she shouted over her shoulder, eyes blazing like a feral hound's. She cursed at Tarsigh, spit on him, removed her right hand, balled it into a fist, and began pummeling.

Tarsigh blocked with his left forearm and managed to wriggle out and onto his side, twisting from her grip and covering with both arms as Aladhra let loose a flurry of blows.

Tarsigh felt her weight leave him. He dared to glance up; Aladhra stepped back and launched a vicious kick that cleared his cover and struck him square in the forehead, setting the world spinning.

He barely registered Braxx grasping Aladhra in a bear hug while she kicked wildly, screaming. "Stop!" Braxx was

110

saying. "Aladhra, stop! STOP!"

Tarsigh was slowly regaining his senses. There was a hand on his shoulder. He turned to see Striker, kneeling, one hand to his ear. "There's a message coming through from Jepps. Hostiles incoming."

"Collective?" Braxx asked, still holding Aladhra, who had at last fallen silent.

"No," Striker answered, looking up. "Onslaught."

CHAPTER 15

Bloodied and still somewhat foggy-headed, Tarsigh made his way to the bridge. *The Onslaught...*

The Onslaught was a band of Ridgerunners known for attacking relentlessly in overwhelming numbers. They utilized any and all weapons, high or low tech, descending on their enemies like a locust swarm. And they were here to claim that one-billion-chit bounty.

Tarsigh immediately issued a code red and ordered shields raised. He had been followed by Aladhra, Braxx, Striker, and Findlay, and all five sub-captains.

Each of them had argued vehemently to return to their respective ships, but to do so would require lowering the

Skipjack's shields, which Tarsigh wasn't prepared to do. Yet. At least they had kept a precautionary six drones at a distance from the fleet, just in case some emergency necessitated them swapping out.

Findlay relieved Jepps at the nav station while Tarsigh approached the observation window, silently. The enemy gathered outside, but the real battle was taking place *inside* the captain. His heart ached at Aladhra's outburst. There would be a great deal of explaining required on his part . . . *if* they survived. Meanwhile, his crew awaited orders.

"They don't know what we can do," he said at last. "And that may be our only chance."

The Onslaught had the Pack surrounded with smaller fighters—most of which were cruisers retrofitted with plasma guns—weaving through the debris field while the larger vessels established a perimeter.

"Send all our drones outside their perimeter," Tarsigh said. "Do it carefully; take advantage of their chaos."

"Aye," Striker answered.

Tarsigh turned to face the sub-captains. "Once we've skipped, we'll lower shields. You can return to your ships then," he said. "Or you can stay and fight here."

"If I die, it'll be aboard the *Rapier*," Sub-Captain Kring stated. This sentiment was echoed among the others . . . all save Sub-Captain Bloom, who stood with his hands balled beneath his chin, eyes darting among the frenzy of ships beyond the window and the impact bursts blossoming against the *Skipjack's* shields.

How had the Onslaught found them? For them to target this particular scrap field among all the others that existed—indeed, among all other possible pirate hideaways in the system—seemed unlikely.

Someone had sent them a message.

Bloom. Many spans ago, Tarsigh had heard a rumor that long before he had come to join the Pack, Bloom had been a member of the Onslaught. It hadn't really mattered at the time; every member of the Pack had their history, and Bloom had been faithful. Until now.

Tarsigh decided to keep his revelation to himself. Though the Onslaught's timing was catastrophic, with all five sub-captains aboard the *Skipjack*, in one sense it was good that he could keep an eye on Bloom. Bloom may have been former Onslaught, but his crew was not. The *Harrier* crew had existed before Bloom came on board; he had only assumed command of the ship three spans ago.

Had Bloom known when the Onslaught would arrive? If not, his plan might have been to jettison himself in a lifepod and join his former comrades. If he *was* aware of their arrival time, he would use the transport to achieve the same result when Tarsigh lowered the shields. Either way, his plan would now be forfeit.

"Bloom, I require your counsel," Tarsigh said.

The big man's eyes widened. "My counsel?" he said.

"That's right. Remaining sub-captains, return to your transports and await my go."

The sub-captains departed.

Wiping blood from under his nose, Tarsigh shot a pained look to Aladhra. She stared back defiantly, then without a word stalked off to her station.

Bloom approached and said quietly, "I'd much rather be among my men, Captain. I don't know how I can—"

"I've never gone against the Onslaught," Tarsigh said,

pulling up a tactical hologram. "I have reason to believe you have more knowledge of their tactics than I do." Tarsigh smiled at the other man, whose face drooped now as if the skin might fall off the bone.

"Shields at 85 percent," Braxx reported.

All of the other ships in the fleet currently had their shields raised as well, and would be taking seemingly endless bombardment, rapidly weakening their shield integrity. At least all Pack vessels had completed their repairs.

Just in time to get hammered again, Tarsigh mused.

"All sub-captains have reported in from their transports," Gungan informed.

"Good," Tarsigh said. Bloom had moved away from the captain, wringing his hands, eyes fixed on the tactical map.

"Uh-oh," Striker said.

Tarsigh turned, frowning. "What do you mean, 'uh-oh'?"

"Fighters targeted one of our drones. Destroyed it."

Tarsigh cursed bitterly. With one drone down, only five were capable of skipping outside the perimeter. If more drones were destroyed, that number would decrease further. Tarsigh knew that whatever ships stayed inside the perimeter would take the heaviest damage, and he was unwilling to force that sacrifice on any vessel other than his own.

"Tactical," he said.

"Done," Gungan replied.

"All ships, ready weapons. Skip immediately and then acquire targets. Repeat: skip immediately. For the time being, your sub-captains will remain aboard the *Skipjack*." Tarsigh and the sub-captains would now have to rely on the competence of their seconds-in-command for charge of their respective vessels. They had no time to return the sub-captains without risking losing their ships in the crossfire.

Tarsigh turned to Gungan. "Tell the sub-captains to return to bridge," he said.

"Shields at 70 percent," Braxx reported.

"Remaining Pack ships skipped successfully," Striker reported.

"Good. Gungan, put me on speakers."

"You're on," Gungan replied.

"Crew, this is your captain. Five of our vessels have skipped outside the enemy perimeter. One of our drones was destroyed, meaning one of us had to stay behind. I made the choice that it would be us. We'll hold on as long as possible, but when our shields are spent, they will throw everything they have at us, and they *will* board us. Our sister ships are going to pound them from all sides and will have the element of surprise, but for those of us on board, things are about to get dire. Pack vessels have only been boarded twice in the past twelve cycles, and both times we emerged on top. We're in for one hell of a fight, but I have no doubt that at the end of this, we'll be the ones still breathing." Tarsigh finished with the Pack credo: "Strength from within."

CHAPTER 16

Shields at 60," Braxx reported.

Tarsigh slapped a hand on Bloom's shoulder, causing the other man to jump. "What do you think, Bloom? What all will they throw at us? Any surprises?"

Bloom's eyes roved all around the bridge, projecting the air of a trapped animal.

"I don't know," he said. "I assume they'll use everything they've got. All ships large and small."

"Aye," Tarsigh answered.

And what Bloom failed to mention was that the Onslaught had also been known to get close and use individuals in pressure suits and thruster packs to cut through hulls.

As Tarsigh watched, the swarm of red dots on the tactical map began dispersing. Though no doubt confused, they were diverting their attention from the *Skipjack*, readjusting now to face the immediate threats of the Pack ships that had skipped outside the Onslaught perimeter.

"Ready all weapons," Tarsigh commanded.

"Aye," Braxx replied.

It was time to get in the fight.

"Weapons ready," Braxx reported.

They needed to shift the Onslaught's attention back to them.

"On my mark, drop shields and cut loose on all nearby targets. Keep a look out for the busters and seekers and target them with plasma rounds if you can."

"Right," Braxx said.

Tarsigh looked to Aladhra. She glanced his way with cold detachment. He then looked at Bloom, who had made his way back toward the control stations. If the sub-captain was going to make a move, it would be soon after the shields went down.

Tarsigh took a deep breath. "Mark," he said.

The shields came down, and Bloom acted almost immediately, making a beeline for the bridge exit. When Tarsigh came after him, Bloom spun, drawing his magnetic revolver from a hip holster. The captain closed the distance and grabbed at the wrist, causing Bloom's arm to swing in the direction of the nav station. Findlay threw up his arms for a shield just as the weapon discharged. The bullet struck Findlay's prosthetic arm at an angle and ricocheted.

The ship rocked from multiple impacts as Striker and

Aladhra both rushed over. Striker was quicker and grasped the sub-captain's gun arm, pointing it down; Bloom fired off two more shots as Tarsigh let go of the wrist and landed a heavy punch to the man's chin, causing his knees to buckle beneath him.

Aladhra went directly to Findlay. "Are you hurt?" she asked.

"No," he replied, grinning widely. "New arm saved me!"

She turned then to Tarsigh and shouted, "What is this?" No doubt she assumed that this had been some kind of betrayal on *his* part rather than Bloom's.

Striker wrenched the gun from Bloom's grip as plasma bursts from the forward battery lit up the observation window behind them. The sub-captain sat on the floor, leaning on one elbow, dazed from the blow. The bridge doors opened to allow back the other four sub-captains, who came in with confused expressions and surrounded the current center of attention.

"It was him that set the Onslaught on us," Tarsigh said. And then, to Bloom: "You were one of them once, weren't you?"

Tarsigh knelt and slapped Bloom. "I said, you were one of the Onslaught once, weren't you? You sold us out."

Bloom looked around to the gathered faces and said, "One billion chits is a lot of money. Plenty o' you woulda done the same."

"They *didn't* do the same," Tarsigh said. "You did. And you'll get locked out for it. But first . . . Auric, Kring," Tarsigh looked up. "You know where the brig is?"

"I do," Kring answered.

"Take him," Tarsigh ordered, then stood and returned

his attention to the tactical map, where the red dots had returned, forming a deadly net around the *Skipjack*.

The ship swayed from a missile impact to the starboard side.

"Buster got through, opened a hole in the docking bay," Braxx said.

Aladhra hurried back to her station as the slender sub-captain, Auric, picked up Bloom's weapon then assisted Kring in hoisting the traitor to his feet.

"I'm showing transports," Aladhra said. "And smaller readings . . . dozens of them."

"Jumpers," Tarsigh replied. These would be the thruster-pack pirates, exiting the transports, piloting themselves to positions on the outer hull and attempting to cut their way in or sneak in through already-existing breaches. "Tactical," he said.

"On," replied Gungan.

"Response teams, look sharp. We got the enemy breaking down our door. Details incoming. Captain out." Tarsigh looked away from the tactical map. Intent on resolving the crisis at hand *and* breaking past the tension between them, Tarsigh turned and said, "Aladhra, identify existing breaches and feed assignments to response crews. Jepps, you're with Aladhra. Look for new breaches as soon as they open and inform remaining crews."

"Bard, you feel like manning the battle station?" Tarsigh asked.

"Happy to," the aged sub-captain answered.

"Good," Tarsigh said. "Braxx, time for you to suit up. I want you and Striker on breach defense."

"Not a problem," Striker answered.

"Gladly," Braxx said, joining Striker on his way out.

"I want to join a response team," Gordo exclaimed.

"Do it," Tarsigh responded.

"I'm going as well," Aladhra said. "Assignments have been given. Jepps will take over my station. I'll be on comms."

Aladhra headed for the doors without waiting for an answer. Tarsigh wanted to stop her, to tell her that he was worried for her, but he knew better. She would do what she had set her mind on.

"Be careful," he called after her as the bridge doors slid closed.

Tarsigh turned back as the ship shuddered.

Bard reported from his station: "Buster got through, but I killed the seeker. Still, we're sustaining heavy damage. Won't last long at this rate."

Looking at the tactical map, Tarsigh eyed the smaller red dots that represented the additional jumpers leaving the transports, attempting to latch onto the *Skipjack* like lampreys on a shark.

"Gungan, tactical," Tarsigh said.

"On," Gungan replied.

"This is Tarsigh. All ships report status."

One by one, the Pack vessels reported in. The element of surprise had certainly worked in their favor, and they had inflicted heavy damage. All seemed optimistic, but it was clear that victory would not come quickly. It was to be a war of attrition, wearing down the Onslaught while the *Skipjack* weathered the storm.

Behind the captain, sub-captains Auric and Kring stepped into the control room. "Bloom's secured," Auric said.

"Good," Tarsigh responded.

Through the observation window, among the debris, he glimpsed a massive shell—the roughly cylindrical hull of an old colony transport, open on both ends but almost fully intact all around.

"How tight a fit you think it'd be inside that hull?" Tarsigh asked the sub-captains, pointing out the window.

"I think we could make it," Kring answered.

"Scanning," Jepps called from Aladhra's station. Then: "We could fit, with a bit of room leftover."

"Findlay, get us there," Tarsigh said.

"Aye," Findlay replied.

The shell cover wouldn't last for very long against the firepower being levied against them, but at least it would give them a brief respite, and the smaller fighters wouldn't be able to maneuver in the cramped space. Alternatively, Tarsigh could order shields reactivated, but then their attackers would all go back to attacking the remaining Pack vessels and what little advantage they had would be lost. The hull tactic might at least retain the Onslaught's interest. But that left the problem of the dozens of jumpers all over the ship, attempting to cut their way in.

Response teams would be occupied with those who had already made it in, unlikely to have time for donning thrusters and engaging those on the outside. He needed a more immediate solution that wouldn't drain manpower.

A thought hit him.

He punched a button on the captain's seat. "Braxx, can you get grappling drones outside and hand off control to command three in about thirty seconds?"

"Not a problem," Braxx's voice replied over the speakers.

To Kring, Tarsigh said, "I want you on command three

controlling those grapplers."

"Sir," Kring replied and rushed to Striker's station.

Sub-Captain Auric stepped up to Tarsigh's side, hands clasped behind him. "I must admit this strategy is . . . unique."

"Unique's all well and good. Let's just hope it's effective."

A shadow fell over the observation window as the *Skipjack* eased into the immense shell. Findlay continued minimal thrust until they were all the way in, where the larger ships and transports were temporarily shut out, save for fore and aft.

Braxx's voice came over the speakers. "Grappling drones are out. Command three has control."

"Confirmed," Kring said.

"Alright then," Tarsigh commented. "Let's start scraping barnacles off the hull."

CHAPTER 17

Braxx had an idea of what might have happened to make Aladhra snap. It must have been something said at the trial. Both he and Tarsigh had known a day like this might come . . . For now, his greatest hope was that neither Aladhra nor Tarsigh would die while she bore such hatred for him. And he was determined to lay down his own life, if necessary, to ensure their survival. The Vulcan armor would assist greatly in that aim, but only if he stayed focused and acted with purpose and precision. With this in mind, he barreled down the corridor on his way to join Response Team Three at the closest breach, in docking bay two.

Based on what he had pieced together from the comm chatter, the response team had pinned down a group of invading Onslaught on the flight deck.

When Braxx entered the upper deck of the bay, he visually confirmed this assumption. The response team, in full jury rig, had brought cargo crates from storerooms and erected them for cover while they exchanged fire with the attackers, who had taken up two separate positions: a pair of pirates behind the *Traveler* cruiser, and two more behind a smaller transport.

The gaping hole in the bay doors had assuredly resulted in loss of pressure at first, but the ships were magnetically secured to the flight deck, so they had remained in position. And now, Braxx and everyone else could move freely because the pressure in the bay had equalized.

Braxx knew immediately what must be done. As the battle was currently being fought, no significant change could be expected in the short term. Each side would continue trading shots and both sides were firing from cover. The Pack had a slight advantage in the higher ground, but that alone wouldn't be enough to shift the tide.

"Team Three, keep at it," Braxx said over comms as he entered the nearest lift and descended to the flight deck. Once there, he engaged the Vulcan's servos and charged out, knowing the suit could withstand most firepower the intruders would bring to bear.

Moving diagonally across the deck, Braxx soon had a line of sight on the pirates at the *Traveler*. They fired centrifugal sling guns; bullets ricocheted furiously off the Vulcan armor as Braxx raised his tri-barrel gun and unloaded what amounted to a nearly solid wall of rounds that bisected the torsos of both men in seconds.

He hurried on, angling for position on the next pirate group. One of the men peeked his head out—a deadly mistake as Braxx's retinal targeting sensors tracked his eye movement and locked on the enemy. A heads-up reticle turned red and everything above the pirate's shoulders was almost instantly gone, vanishing in a misty red cloud of blood and solid matter.

The last intruder ran out and engaged his thrusters, flying upward and directly into the response team's line of fire. His lifeless, ventilated body fell to the flight deck seconds later.

"Papa Bear, behind you," one of the response team members said.

Braxx turned to see a jumper coming in through the breach, holding a contraption half his size, a device that Braxx immediately recognized. He stormed to the intruder's position, the resulting collision launching the man off his feet. Braxx stepped up and fired point-blank into his enemy's chest, effectively obliterating the upper half of the pirate's body and punching a sizable hole in the deck. He then rushed to the device and carried it back to the lift.

Once the lift doors had closed, he hit the emergency stop button and worked quickly; after removing the suit's left glove, he carefully disabled the device's firing mechanism. With the glove back on, he got the lift moving again to the upper deck. As soon as the door opened, through the suit's external speakers he told one of the response team members to take the device to waste disposal.

With the weapon out of his hands, he announced somberly on the tactical channel: "Everyone be aware, one of 'em tried to use a spreader. I disabled it, but be on the lookout."

Sub-Captain Gordo of the *Monolith* heard Braxx's proclamation as he closed in on Response Team One's location, and he cursed under his breath. It wasn't bad enough that they were under siege by rival Ridgerunners, no, these pirates were using spreaders.

"Spreader" was the familiar name used to describe the Deep Penetrating Radiological Device, a bomb capable of releasing high levels of concentrated radiation over a far-reaching radius, enough to radiate an entire beta-class vessel with lethal doses. The levels were typically not enough to kill immediately; the primary effect of the bomb was psychological, as it was known that exposure to the radiation would set in motion an irreversible and excruciating physical decline—including vomiting, crippling stomach pain, and cellular breakdown—ending in a gruesome demise, usually in less than a cycle. It was a weapon of terror, its very mention striking fear into even the hardest of hearts.

Gordo heard an explosion as he exited the lift for deck two, one of the *Skipjack's* three crew decks. His first thought was that maybe a spreader had detonated, but as he saw the flash and witnessed a body fly out from the intersecting corridor ahead, he came to the conclusion that it was most likely an arc grenade.

Smoke was billowing out from the passage as well, but Gordo suspected this was the work of a smoke grenade meant to obscure the infiltrator's movements and not caused by the arc.

Crawling on hands and knees, Gordo cursed the terrible fit of his pressure suit. His suit aboard the *Monolith* had been altered specifically for his size. He peeked around the corner and into the corridor. Smoke obscured nearly the entirety of the passage. Rather than firing blindly, he decided to crawl further in and wait.

He came to an obstruction, realizing as he probed that it was a fallen response team member. Whispering a brief salutation to the deceased soldier, he settled in next to the body and remained still.

For the first minute, the only sound was his own breathing. Then, the suit's external mics picked up shuffling noises as the enemy advanced.

Gordo held the sling gun close to his body, angling the barrel upward, attempting to appear dead as the smoke began to clear.

With his head cocked to the side, laying against the bulkhead, he peered through the faceplate to see three figures emerging. The waist-high smoke made it appear as if the Ridgerunners were fording a river. Gordo held his breath as the first of them drew near. The man fired a single bullet into the body Gordo was lying next to. Before the pirate could fire again, Gordo squeezed off a burst, center-mass. The man dropped; Gordo arced his arm over both fallen bodies, spraying the hallway left to right.

A much larger figure appeared above the haze. This one dropped to its belly; an instant later, Gordo was rolling onto his shoulder and then stomach as the powerful opponent shoved *both* dead bodies at once with prodigious force.

A mad scramble followed as Gordo attempted to recover and still maintain a low profile, but the much larger pirate was on him, one hand locked around Gordo's gun wrist, angling the weapon away while the intruder shoved the barrel of his own gun against Gordo's faceplate. Gordo shut his eyes; gunfire sounded.

But he was somehow still alive. He felt the pressure on his wrist release, opened his eyes to see the massive form fall to the side, joining the pile of bodies. Another figure stepped into view, from the same direction Gordo had come. Through the faceplate he saw his savior's face: Aladhra.

"Man, am I happy to see you," he voiced through the external speakers.

Aladhra's head whipped up in response to the sound of footfalls, the noise of one or more persons running in the opposite direction. Aladhra returned her gaze to Gordo, held out her hand, and said, "Job's not done yet."

"All ships, status," Tarsigh said over the tactical channel.

"This is *Death Rattle*," a voice replied. "We've disabled three Onslaught vessels and fended off jumpers."

Next to the captain, Sub-Captain Auric lifted his chin proudly.

"This is *Monolith*," another voice announced. "We have multiple breaches and are battling intruders, but I think their numbers are fairly small. I hope." The interim sub-captain didn't sound too sure.

The *Harrier* reported in next: "We've sustained minimal

damage and kept jumpers off of us. Been on the move and neutralized one of their larger vessels." That sounded promising.

"This is *Talon*," a voice reported. "We're barely hanging in, but we've done a lot of damage. Destroyed a handful of their fighters and killed the only jumpers who made it on board."

Tarsigh threw a look over his shoulder at Bard, who glanced back, nodded, and returned his attention to the battle station. A few seconds passed while Tarsigh waited for *Rapier's* report.

"Grappling drone just took out another jumper," Kring announced. The drones' arms were being used to carry off and crush the would-be intruders. An inelegant solution that was nonetheless proving effective.

Just then an Onslaught jumper appeared high up just outside the observation window.

"Kring, bring one of those drones around front," Tarsigh said.

"Got him," Kring answered.

The jumper stuck a wad of gel onto the window. He then retrieved an arc grenade and armed it. Before he could place the grenade in the gel, however, a grappling drone swept across. It closed its arms around the jumper and sped off. Seconds later a bright flash signaled the demise of both the drone and the jumper.

"Well," Kring said, "lost a drone but that jumper got the surprise of his life."

"Or death," Findlay said, sounding amused.

Soft chuckles sounded throughout the command deck. Tarsigh, however, was not laughing. He was concerned about the fact that *Rapier* had not called in.

"*Rapier*, status," Tarsigh said.

No answer. Kring stopped chuckling. Just as Tarsigh was about to ask again for a status report, a frazzled voice came over the speakers. "This is acting sub-captain Larabee of the *Rapier*," it said. "Regret to report . . . one of 'em used a spreader on us. We got him. . . but the device went off."

Silence pervaded the bridge. Kring's shoulders had slumped, and Tarsigh thought if the big man wasn't in the midst of defending the *Skipjack* through the grappling drones, he might collapse. The sub-captain shot a look at Tarsigh that said it all: those men were all dead, it was just a matter of time.

Tarsigh answered Larabee. "Acknowledged. Keep fighting. Don't give up. We'll assess once the battle is finished."

"Strength from within," Larabee answered.

"Strength from within," Tarsigh replied, and it was all he could do to keep his voice even.

CHAPTER 18

Aladhra emerged from the smoke at the end of the hall, taking a quick glance to make sure Gordo was following. They took up positions on either side of the doors leading to Cargo Bay One. Gordo gave Aladhra a nod, and she hit the button for the door. No gunfire streamed through, so Gordo rushed across the threshold. Aladhra followed an instant later.

The large, open bay contained dozens of carts, crates, and containers ranging in size from one to three meters square or as much as five meters high. Some were stacked haphazardly, while larger crates had been lined up in rows. The whole of the assembly provided for infinite hiding places.

Through hand signals, Aladhra directed Gordo to take one side of the room while she took the other. Slowly, crate by crate, the two of them began clearing the space.

When she had progressed halfway across the bay, a noise attracted her attention. The sound of someone making a run for it?

She spotted Gordo rushing off at the opposite end of the aisle she was searching, and she hurried to cover him. Gunfire erupted as she emerged from a cluster of crates into an open space. Gordo had shot an Onslaught member, who was down and bleeding on the floor. The smaller man continued moving in to finish the job. There were more potential crates to hide behind in the corner of the room, however. Aladhra bolted to the far wall and aimed her weapon along it; she saw a foot disappear from view, too late to fire. "Gordo!" she yelled over the tactical channel as the Ridgerunner came out on the other side of the large crates. She was too late: the enemy fired twice, one-handed, both shots striking Gordo dead-center. The small man fell and was still.

Aladhra fired, striking the intruder high on the right side of the chest. Only then, as he turned, did she realize that he held an arc grenade, already activated. Looking to her left, she sighted the door of a storeroom. With a quick slap she hit the button and immediately jumped in as the door opened. She heard the grenade bouncing on the floor, saw it come into view just as the pocket door slid shut.

There was a thundering BOOM! on the other side. The floor shook and the door bowed inward with a metallic groan.

Aladhra got up, ran over, and hit the button. A futile buzz of machinery sounded; the door was far too warped to slide open.

With a roar of frustration Aladhra kicked, then pounded. It was no use. Panting from her exertion, she looked around the room. It was a mid-sized storeroom, roughly five by eight meters, with a small air vent. She removed her helmet and said into the earpiece: "This is Aladhra. Gordo's down in Cargo Bay One. I'm stuck in a storeroom, can't get to him. There might be one hostile still in play."

"I read ya', Ladhi, hang tight," Braxx said. "You okay?"

"Yeah, I'm fine," Aladhra answered.

"This is Summers, Response Team Three. We're close by. Be there as quick as we can."

"Copy," Aladhra said, setting her helmet on a nearby table and hoisting herself to a seated position atop it. She rubbed her face, balled her hands into fists, cursing herself for not being fast enough, aware enough, to save Gordo.

She pulled her legs up, tucked her knees and wrapped her arms around them, and waited.

Striker hadn't had a chance to use his repulsor gun yet in this battle—which was a shame because it was his favorite new toy—but he had eliminated three Onslaught infiltrators. When the call came over comms that a small group of them had broken in and were making their way to the missile stores, he recognized an opportunity and immediately contacted Braxx.

Striker asked Jepps to close the blast door behind the encroaching enemy, and his request was granted. He waited at a corridor connecting to the starboard side passage—the last one before the storeroom at the aft end of the ship, deck three.

He had no arc grenades, but he wouldn't need one, not if this worked the way he hoped it would. As the Onslaught crew approached, Striker coordinated with Braxx over comms, then stepped out and activated the repulsor gun. Its energy barrier fanned out as the mini-thruster projectile sped it down the passage, collecting the enemy squad, piling them up, sweeping them with irresistible force toward the blast door.

Where the blast door sealed off the longitudinal starboard corridor, a transverse corridor connected. Here, Braxx waited just as Striker had asked him to, a few meters from the intersection, tri-barrel raised. When the mound of bodies flooded into view, pressed by the repulsor barrier against the blast door, Braxx disgorged a full load of ammo from all three barrels into that stack of people, maintaining a four-thousand-round per second rate of fire from each barrel over the course of a full twenty seconds. In the end, he had reduced what was once a pile of human beings to a mass confusion of unrecognizable, carnal ruin.

Tarsigh stood, distracted, quietly considering the fact that Aladhra was temporarily isolated and incapacitated.

"Well, I'll be," Auric said next to him.

Tarsigh followed his gaze, to the tactical map.

"I believe we're close to pulling this off," the sub-captain enthused.

And he was right. The enemy numbers were dwindling.

"I show five primary vessels remaining," Bard reported from the battle station.

"Good," Tarsigh replied. The time had come now to press the advantage. "Findlay, take us out of this shell and engage our closest target."

"Heading out now," Findlay replied.

The *Skipjack* broke free of the massive hull and took a heading toward the closest Onslaught ship, an overhauled beta-class destroyer. It was already badly damaged, taking a heavy pummeling from both the *Harrier* and the *Talon*.

With *Skipjack* adding to the bombardment, the Onslaught ship was quickly neutralized.

It was at that time the transports began returning to the remaining primary vessels.

"We have them on the run," Auric observed.

"I show no more jumpers," Jepps reported.

Outside. But what about inside?

While he considered this, the remaining Onslaught ships engaged thrusters and departed at maximum speed. Findlay whooped, Bard hooted, Kring pounded his chest. Jepps whistled, Auric pumped his fist. Even Gungan managed a smile and a nod.

Tarsigh hit a button on his chair. "Response teams, estimated number of enemies on board."

One by one the response teams indicated that there were no enemy jumpers at large. "Keep looking," Tarsigh said. "Check every hole. And someone confirm Sub-Captain

Gordo's condition."

Braxx's voice came over the speakers. "I've just arrived at the cargo bay." He hesitated. Then: "Confirmed. Sub-Captain Gordo is gone."

Tarsigh pushed past the tightening in his gut and said, "Understood." There was no doubt: the Collective's strategy of using Ridgerunners against the Pack was wearing them down. One good sub-captain gone, another turned . . . and an entire ship filled with men and women living on borrowed time. How many more would die before the Pack was able to even attempt its "crippling blow" against the Collective?

He had been turning something over in his mind, and came at last to a decision, a terrible choice; but he believed now more than ever that it was the right one.

"Get me a direct line to Striker and Braxx only," he said.

"Done," Gungan answered.

"Striker, Braxx, I want you back on the bridge."

Braxx responded, "Sir, we need to get Aladhra out of—"

"She's in no immediate danger," Tarsigh replied. "Make no further attempts to free her and report to me immediately. That's an order."

A few seconds of tense silence followed, broken by Braxx and Striker both finally saying "Aye."

Tarsigh then said, "Gungan, tactical."

Gungan complied.

"All ships: we'll have no time to board enemy vessels. Gather whatever salvage materials you can from what's been destroyed and make ready to skip. All save for the *Rapier*." Tarsigh ignored for the moment the questioning look Kring sent him. "Also, eliminate any remaining jumpers and make a clean sweep of your vessels. Any enemies left on board, lock them out." He then added: "*Monolith* sub-captain report."

"This is *Monolith* Acting Sub-Captain Takashi," a voice returned.

"Takashi, you will inform your crew that Sub-Captain Gordo fell in battle. He died a warrior's death, and he honored us all. As of now, you are the official sub-captain of the *Monolith*. Do you understand?"

A long silence was followed by "We all . . . admired him, sir. I'm not sure that I can—"

"You'll rise to the occasion," Tarsigh said. "And in doing so you'll honor your former captain's memory. Am I clear?"

"Clear, sir."

"*Harrier* sub-captain, report," Tarsigh ordered.

"This is acting sub-captain Katz," a female voice replied.

"Katz, I have bad news regarding your sub-captain, Bloom. Bloom was a traitor who turned against the Pack and brought the Onslaught down on us."

"I . . . can't believe it," Katz answered. "We had no—"

"I know you weren't aware," Tarsigh answered. "Be advised you are now acting sub-captain of the *Harrier*. Sub-Captain Bloom has been taken prisoner and awaits his fate."

Just then Striker and Braxx arrived on the bridge.

"Captain out," Tarsigh said and faced Striker. "Did the drones make it onto that cargo ship?"

"Sir?" Striker answered, frowning.

"Before all of this tore off, we had a meeting. The drones, you were going to program them and send them to the ship leaving Farpost Seven. Did they make it there?"

"Hold just a tick," Striker said, hurrying to his station. A second later he said, "Got confirmation from our contact during the battle. Drones are en route to Mars."

"Good," Tarsigh answered. "I have a message to send to the hauler captain. First, plot us a section of empty space and make ready to skip us there," he ordered.

"Yes, sir," Striker replied.

"Cap, I—" Braxx began, but Tarsigh held up a hand.

"I know you're itching to free Aladhra," he said. "But before you do, there's something very important that you all need to hear."

CHAPTER 19

Condon hoped this little escapade wasn't a colossal waste of time.

The pirate who had approached Folk, that greaseball Spirion, had convinced the Old Man that the Pack would attempt to infiltrate the Inter-Solar News Network's primary broadcasting station, in orbit around Mars.

And so it was that Condon found himself on the red planet. His terrestrial accommodations—a wraparound penthouse near the summit of Olympus Mons—were adequate, but this diversion had taken him away from work, and he doubted the veracity of Spirion's claims. Whether the pirate was lying or not didn't matter; even if he believed wholeheartedly in his supposition, that wouldn't make it more a reality.

If the pirate overpromised and under-delivered, the consequences were on him.

The Ridgerunner's claim was that the Pack had acquired the damning information against the Collective from the Europans and that they would attempt to broadcast it far and wide from ISNN. He also boasted a limited knowledge of, and potential strategy against, the Pack's adopted space-hopping technology.

Folk had insisted that Bullock and Condon be present for the Pack's potential gambit. They had waited for three Martian days with no result. Condon had been making steady use of his sit-in droid for numerous double-booked meetings.

He had just finished one such meeting when a communication came through from Stanley Teller. It was the news Condon had been waiting for: the work on Jeff Kamura's sit-in droid had been completed.

Normally, a sit-in droid's eyes would light up while functioning. Also, the droid had to be manually activated by someone in the room. Condon had ordered Teller to disable the eye-light function and—this had taken more time—to alter the droid for remote activation. The final piece, which Condon had taken care of on his own, was to give himself permission for the droid's use.

Condon looked at the time. It would just now be evening on earth. Kamura would most assuredly still be at work.

Now it was time to see if the seeds he had planted would yield any fruit.

Condon put on his VR headset and gloves, went through

the proper log-ins to access Kamura's droid, and pointed his finger to the hovering activate button.

He had gambled that Kamura, like most executives, kept his droid on a table somewhere in his office. As the scene before his eyes changed, Condon was relieved to see that his gamble had paid off. What Condon was looking at through the goggles was definitely Kamura's office. He was in the corner of the room, almost waist-high, but his gaze was directed toward the back wall. He could hear Kamura typing away at his desk.

This next part, then, would be tricky: Condon turned his head, the slightest fraction to his right, which in turn rotated the head of the droid. He waited, then turned a fraction more; he repeated this process, pausing the connection so he could bring his head forward again, then reactivating and turning his head again, until Kamura at last came into view. The man was looking alternately down and up, fully absorbed in whatever task he was performing.

One more oscillation and Condon was granted a look at Kamura's desk. There, hovering above, was a blue, semi-transparent hologram. It took up nearly the entirety of the space above the desktop. Condon frowned inside the goggles. What he was looking at was a human brain. A bright, flat plane swept across from one lobe to another, lighting up neural pathways as it went. Once it completed a pass, it made another. And another.

And then it dawned on Condon what he was looking at. It was a project his own team had taken a preliminary stab at, before it had been cancelled by Folk.

Not cancelled after all, merely reassigned.

What he was looking at was brain mapping. A million

questions presented themselves. Why had the project been reassigned? Why the secrecy surrounding it? Or, was Bullock undertaking this program on her own? Was it being hidden from the Old Man? Either way, it begged further questions, such as: whose brains were being mapped? To what end goal? The possible applications were numerous. Did this have anything to do with Bullock rendering him unconscious on board the *Spearhead*? More importantly, this led Condon to consider: the brain hovering above Kamura's desk . . .

Did it belong to him?

Aladhra wondered just what in the known worlds could be taking so long.

She hadn't heard anyone working on the door, and her calls over the comm for updates had resulted in vague excuses. Braxx, for some strange reason, had been unreachable.

One hour became two, and Aladhra had begun transmitting irate demands for results over all channels when she finally heard activity on the other side of the door.

A couple engineers cut their way through, unable to answer any of her questions, saying only that Braxx had sent them.

Gordo's body was gone.

Moments later Aladhra was charging onto the bridge. Tarsigh was nowhere to be seen. Neither was Braxx. She strode boldly to within an inch of Striker. "Where's Tarsigh?" Her tone left no room for equivocation.

"He's gone," Striker said.

"Where?"

"I can't say," Striker answered quietly.

"Did we skip?"

"Yeah. We're in the middle of nowhere." Before she could ask another question, Striker said, "Braxx wants to talk to you. Alone. He's waiting outside your cabin."

Aladhra took a look around. The sub-captains were nowhere to be seen. Findlay and Jepps both avoided her gaze.

She cursed all of them and stormed off the bridge.

When she arrived at her cabin, Braxx was sitting against the door. The big man looked up at her with red-rimmed eyes.

"Ladhi," he said, and maneuvered to his feet. "Tarsigh left you a message."

"A message?" She cut in. "He just left? At a time like this?"

"Ladhi—"

"I've had it with him!" Aladhra spat. "I heard the transmissions, from Koros's trial. The *Redoubt*. I know what happened! That Tarsigh—"

"You don't know what happened!" Braxx said, loud enough that Aladhra leaned back, a look of mild astonishment on her face. Braxx had never, ever yelled at her in all the years she had known him. Even on occasions when she herself felt she had most likely deserved it, he had never yelled at her.

"I *do* know what happened." The big man's eyes locked on hers. "I was there, and I know," he said more quietly. "We all agreed to keep the truth from you. That it was for the best. We wanted you to think of your father as a hero, but that's not the truth, Ladhi. It's time you know."

Without really knowing why, Aladhra had begun crying.

146

It was if some part of her was already reacting to what Braxx was about to say.

"Your father, he was workin' both sides," Braxx said. "We don't know at what point the Collective got to him, but when it came time to take out the *Vigilant*, we had suspected for a while. Cole disarmed the bombs we had set. But because we'd been suspicious of him we had wired them to rearm remotely. Once he'd done what he'd done though, we knew. And that's why Tarsigh chose to leave him."

Aladhra thought about the transmission the prosecutor had played. Her dad, yelling, calling them cowards, saying he would give them something to die for. What was it *he* had died for, in the end? The Collective? She never would have thought it possible, but then . . . how well had she really known him?

"Like I said, we thought it best for you to remember him differently," Braxx said. "But there are reasons that you need to know this now. Listen to the message Tarsigh left for you. And keep in mind what I've said. When you're ready, come find me."

Braxx walked away. Aladhra entered her cabin, her mind still reeling from what the big man had told her. Sitting there in the middle of her floor was the data cube.

Tarsigh had left it. Left it to her.

Aladhra stood completely still, trying to process what she had just been told. Where shock and outrage or, hell, even denial *should* have existed, there was in this moment only quiet acceptance. Had she known, on some level? Had some part of her *always* known, ever since she was little? Was that the true root of her rage?

A blinking light on her monitor informed of a waiting

message.

Aladhra pulled up a chair, not sure if she was ready to hear more or not. Finally she said, "Message, play."

CHAPTER 20

Captain Bryce Fletcher had his reasons for undermining the Collective: taxes, regulations, restrictions... working as an independent operator allowed him and his freight enterprise a certain degree of freedom, yes, but it also meant that he would only ever be as successful as the suits *allowed* him to be. And that was a plateau he had reached years ago; around the very same time he had begun supplementing his income by smuggling contraband for various Ridgerunners throughout the system. When opportunities presented themselves for him to aid former rebels, even better. He would love nothing better than to see the Collective overthrown. This desire, however, was always balanced with caution. He valued his life, his crew, and his ship, in that order, above all else.

When Captain Tarsigh of the Pack had asked Fletcher to smuggle six sphere drones to MARSA, he had readily agreed. The pay was good, and the risk, in his estimation, was low. Thus far, his instincts had proven correct. His hauler, *Star Runner*, had made its way past MARSA traffic control screening without incident. The vessel had taken a slight detour before pulling in to dock, and Fletcher was ready to order the release of the drones as requested when the chief mate informed him that a message had come in over the secure channel.

Once the communication was patched through to his earpiece, he listened, then asked the comms officer to put him through to the forward airlock. There, two crew members had deposited the Pack's spheres and activated them.

"Just one," Fletcher announced to the men in the airlock.

"Say again?" a crewman's voice replied on the main speaker.

"Shut the others off and haul 'em in," the captain said. "We're just sending out one drone."

"Copy."

Fletcher strode to the bridge observation window. Within a few seconds, he spotted the single drone, now just one among hundreds in orbit around Mars, going about various tasks.

This one in particular, however, made a course straight for the ISNN Broadcast Station.

———◆———

Captain Bartlett considered himself fortunate.

He was, after all, still alive even after the loss of his ship *Imperious* to the Pack. His entire command crew had not been so lucky. They had all paid the ultimate price for failure. Bartlett himself had only escaped termination because of his lineage: his father traced an ancestry back to the old families, the founders, those who had been on the "ground floor" of the Collective. Nepotism, thankfully, was alive and well despite the Collective's zero-tolerance policy regarding failure.

So Bartlett had been given a second chance. Not as captain of a ship, but rather as a commander of the primary mobile strike team assembled to neutralize the Pack. It was a worthy appointment, but he desperately needed a "win," as the suits would say. Pedigree or no, a second failure would surely end with his severance.

It was Bartlett's hope that his redemption would come by way of this traitorous Ridgerunner Spirion. The man's claims were certainly bold enough. And though his presence was a constant annoyance, actionable intelligence would certainly make the irritation worthwhile.

Bartlett did wish, however, that the slovenly, battle-scarred individual would stay in his assigned office. The entire strike team had been granted ISNN offices to barrack in while they awaited any sign of their enemy. And while Bartlett and the members of his team had made use of the station's gymnasium showers for their daily hygiene, Spirion had apparently felt no such compulsion, a predicament that wouldn't be nearly as problematic if the man didn't insist on staying glued to Bartlett's side.

They sat now in the station's green room, a dining and leisure area normally reserved for visiting celebrities. ISNN broadcasts played on myriad screens while Bartlett sipped a coffee. Spirion was sprawled out on a table nearby, staring at the ceiling.

Bartlett was preparing to suggest that the pest go and get some sleep when the conference communicator on the table in front of him lit up. "Commander Bartlett, this is MARSA traffic control. We have a drone with no identifier, ninety-one centimeters in diameter."

Bartlett had told traffic control to monitor all drones anywhere within the vicinity of the station.

"It's currently positioned one hundred and fifty meters outside the Broadcasting Station," the controller concluded.

Spirion bolted up and rushed over to the table. His smile was practically salacious.

"Make ready," he said. "They're here."

On the monitor, Tarsigh wiped a hand down his face. The skin under his red eyes was puffy.

Aladhra waited for the image to speak.

"I'm recording this before boarding the *Rapier*, where we'll proceed to Saturn and use its gravity well to match for Mars when we skip. *Rapier* got hit with a spreader; Braxx, he'll tell you all about it."

The cobra on his neck slithered out of sight as the tiger reared up, fangs bared, claws poised.

"You'll want to know why I'm doing what I've decided

to do. The uncomfortable truth is, we can't hide forever. Not with the Collective *and* every Ridgerunner in the system out for us. Garth, Bloom, they've shown that trust and loyalty only go so far when there's one billion chits in the offing. With what happened on board the *Rapier*, the crew's on borrowed time, and they know it. I've asked them to embark on one final mission. I'm leading it . . . because I can't ask these men and women to do this alone, to do something I wouldn't do myself. But there's another reason, one that might make more sense after I've said my piece . . ."

Aladhra's hands covered her mouth as she leaned in. "One final mission?" she whispered. Did Tarsigh not intend to come back?

"First, about your dad: whatever it is you might have heard, whatever was said at the trial, I know it set you off. In fact, my head's still sore. Feels like I got hit with a battering ram. Anyway, whatever you heard, what I'm tryin' to say is: you don't know what you think you know. I'm not sayin' that to steam you; it's just fact. There are things Braxx and I didn't tell you. That was a decision I made a long time ago, for your own good. You're just gonna have to trust me on that. If I had it to do all over again, well, that's something I wouldn't change."

Tarsigh sucked in a long breath and let it out.

"But there's plenty I would change. I made a lot of mistakes, raising you all those years. I know it wasn't easy. I know I'm a pain and for some reason, when it comes to you, what I say and do just doesn't come across the way I want it to. So I want to be clear now, and tell you something I should have told you a long time ago . . ." He looked steadily now at the camera. "The years I spent with you were the happiest, best years of my life. Before that I was . . . incomplete. Like there was a big hole right in the middle of me and I didn't know what was missing or how to fill it. And then you came along and that was it; that was the answer. *You* were the answer."

Aladhra swallowed the lump forming in her throat.

"I didn't know the first thing about being a dad, and I'm pretty sure I hashed it just about every way possible. But understand something: I love you. I'd do anything for you. Anything to protect you. I decided a long time ago that if the situation called for it, I would die for you, without hesitation or regret."

Tears fell freely now, spilling down Aladhra's cheeks and over her fingers.

"You brought out the best in me, and you're a part of me I could never do without. That's why I don't want you following. And that's the other reason I'm doing what I'm doing . . . because I need you to live. A long, healthy, meaningful life. No matter what happens to me. They won't take me alive, I can tell you that, but if what I have planned doesn't work . . . me being removed from the equation might be enough for them to drop the bounty."

Aladhra shook her head as the full force of Tarsigh's words hit her. He *didn't* plan to come back. This was a suicide mission.

On the screen, the captain took in another breath followed by a long exhale. "Okay, that was a lot, I know. But anyway, here we are. I've left you the data cube. I've got a disk I'm gonna use at the news station. Not everything from the cube, not by a long shot, but let's say it's the 'greatest hits'—some of the nastiest, lowest, and most unthinkable atrocities the Collective has committed, and I mean to air it for the whole system to see."

Tarsigh nodded in self-preparation. "We're gonna do everything we can to strike a blow at the Collective, to make this count. But if that doesn't happen . . . I want you to look at file 1456 on the data cube. Keep that in reserve; that alone could be enough to chop the head off the snake. You'll see what I mean. If you use it, be safe and be smart.

"That's it, I'm signing off. Thank you for the joy you've brought me. I love you always. Lead the crew of the *Skipjack* to the best of your ability. Braxx will help, but mostly it's up to you. *You* are the captain now."

CHAPTER 21

Tarsigh stood on the Rapier's bridge, looking out at the rings of Saturn.

He, along with the entire crew, had gone through decontamination and donned jury-rig pressure suits following the spreader attack; it was merely palliative, however, and every single crew member understood that. Tarsigh's pressure suit was only meant to shield him from the effects of the radiation long enough to do what he needed to do.

"If all has gone well, the drone will be in place," Sub-Captain Larabee said at his side.

Tarsigh thought again about Aladhra: had she seen the

message yet? Could she be watching it right now? How would she react? Would she understand?

Kring had certainly *not* understood, when Tarsigh had informed the sub-captain of his plan. It had taken Braxx holding the man back to prevent him from being the one leading this mission.

But he needed to focus, concentrate now on what had to be done.

"Okay," he said. "Let's get ready."

Moments later, he was seated with seven armed crewpersons—the most battle-hardened available—in the cruiser *Arrow*, which sat on the flight deck of the *Rapier's* docking bay. The *Rapier* waited within a designated depth of Saturn's gravity well.

The tech officer's voice came through Tarsigh's headset: "We should be set."

"Depth match?" Tarsigh asked.

"Matched," the officer confirmed.

"Velocity match?" Tarsigh continued.

"Matched," the tech officer reported.

"On my mark," the captain said. "Three . . . two . . . one . . . mark."

Tarsigh knew that out near Mars, as the drone's energy field expanded, if it encountered any obstructions or conditions that would threaten the relocation, it would abort and they would end up going nowhere. He waited, leaning against the back of his seat. This was the farthest skip they had attempted up to this point. Uncharted territory, for him at least.

Tarsigh waited on confirmation from Larabee that they had reached their destination. "We're here," Larabee finally told him in the comm. "We're here, we made it."

Condon sped toward the command post, Commander Bartlett's voice in his ear: "The drone was replaced by a ship, Sigma class, with no identifier. I've locked down all station employees, no one allowed below level two."

Condon could hardly believe what he was hearing. So . . . the pirate traitor was correct after all. "How many vessels?" he asked into the headpiece.

"One so far," Bartlett answered.

Condon slowed as he entered the multi-tiered, open space. Massive hovering tactical displays populated the room. Bullock was standing at one of these, behind an operator, looking over her shoulder at Condon's arrival. He offered her little more than a glance, saying nothing as he walked to a vantage point that allowed him to see the various maps.

Thirteen smaller displays blinked on, each showing a body-cam point of view of a strike team member, the soldier's name, location, and vitals positioned in the upper left. All members of the team were represented, save the Ridgerunner Spirion, who had not been assigned a body cam.

Condon stood and waited, a single, nagging thought perplexing him:

Where were the other pirates?

CHAPTER 22

Aladhra had sat in stunned silence for a protracted period of time following her viewing of Tarsigh's message. For the moment, all of her emotions were dammed up inside her.

She got up, rushed from the room, and moments later swept onto the bridge, beelining for Striker. "Where are the drones? Mars?"

Striker looked over at Findlay, then back to her. "One outside the station. The others . . . Tarsigh sent a message to the *Star Runner* before he left, to only release the one."

"What? Why?"

Braxx entered the bridge and was at her side instantly. "He didn't want you to follow," the big man said.

"I DON'T CARE!" Aladhra yelled back. The dam was bursting now, the emotions flooding. "I don't care, he—he—I didn't get to tell him, I didn't say what I need to say. It's not right! I need to help him! He needs to know—"

Braxx put his hands on her shoulders, but she batted them away.

"No! He doesn't know, he doesn't know . . . because I didn't tell him!"

"He does know," Braxx said quietly. "Why do you think he was so sure you'd follow?"

She whirled on Striker, who recoiled slightly. "Send a message to the *Star Runner* to get those drones out. Now!"

"Ladhi, that's not—" Braxx tried, but she cut him off.

"Do it! That's an order! Do you understand me?" She grabbed Striker by the collar. "Now! Get them out and in position!"

Striker looked to Braxx, who nodded. "Okay," Striker said. "Okay, yeah, you got it."

Aladhra brushed past Braxx and back to the captain's chair.

"I need a status . . . on all the ships. Gungan, put me on tactical."

"Done," he replied.

Braxx, Findlay, and Striker all exchanged looks that Aladhra ignored.

"All vessels, this is . . . Aladhra." She refused to say captain. Not yet. "How soon can you all be in fighting shape?"

"Ladhi, they're not—" Braxx began, but Aladhra held up a hand. One by one, the Pack ships reported in. *Monolith* and *Talon* were the worst off, estimating a full rotation at least before they would be anywhere near battle-ready. *Harrier* and *Death Rattle* reported potential readiness in half that time.

"We'll leave *Monolith* and *Talon* if we have to," Aladhra said when she'd ended the communication. "How about us? Where are we with repairs?" she asked Braxx.

"We took a hell of a beating," he answered. "But we've been working nonstop. Eighteen hours to go, that's just an estimate."

"Cut that in half," Aladhra ordered. "And get me caught up."

The *Arrow* launched from *Rapier's* docking bay, on a direct course to the ISNN broadcast station. Ignoring calls from the station for the vessel to self-identify and state its purpose, the cruiser swept into the bay and flew to the first available visitor's berth.

Tarsigh's centrifugal sling gun made short work of the secured airlock entry. Within seconds the captain and his armed comrades stormed into the receiving atrium. The receptionist was nowhere to be seen. In fact, the entire atrium was deserted . . . or at least appeared to be.

"*Rapier*, report," the captain said into his headpiece, stepping to one side and stopping. He held up a fist, arm at an L, signaling the others to do the same.

"All quiet so far," Larabee responded.

Tarsigh removed his helmet to allow better peripheral vision and scanned the reception area: a meter-high base for the towering holographic broadcast that currently played; the large reception desk; a door behind and to his left, possibly a stairwell; three lifts across from them.

Plenty of places to hide. A great spot for an ambush.

"They know we're here," Tarsigh said as the middle lift announced the car arrival with a ding. Two armed soldiers stepped out from the car, firing railguns.

He recognized the man who stood up from behind the reception desk: it was the captain they had sent out on a lifepod just before they had claimed the data cube. The captain fired a railgun into the nearest of his team, the smart slug punching through the man's torso, exploding out his back and blowing apart just before hitting the wall to Tarsigh's rear.

Gunfire erupted from behind the holo-base to his right, ventilating another of his comrades.

The door behind him opened. Tarsigh spun and cut loose a storm of bullets that stitched across the two exiting soldiers, severing their heads at the neck.

"Fall back on me!" he shouted, retreating toward the door, blocked now by one of the fallen bodies.

He glanced inside: it was a stairwell, as he had thought. Tarsigh provided cover fire, forcing the other captain to duck back behind the reception desk. What was left of Tarsigh's team, now numbering just four, rushed to his position and through the door, the last of them falling to a railgun slug that blew a hole through the center of his chest.

Amid a litany of curses, Tarsigh stepped in and pushed the obstructing soldier's corpse away, allowing the door to close. He moved up two steps and squeezed off a burst into the door's sensor, disabling it.

"Move!" he said, spinning and setting off up the stairs. Then, into his comm: "*Rapier*: plasma rounds. Light this place up."

CHAPTER 23

Condon watched the battle unfold with rapt attention. Two out of twelve of the strike team were dead, a third gravely wounded. Half of the invading party had been killed.

But where were the rest?

"We should move the ships in," Bullock said at his side. He glanced her way. "There should be five more Pack ships out there," he said.

Just then all hell broke loose across the feeds. Unable to access the stairwell door to pursue, the strike team members had rushed back to the lifts. A cacophony blared over the speakers: shattering glass, rending metal, screams as three of the team who didn't make it into the lift were torn apart.

Two of the body cams winked out as the vitals went flat. The third pointed upward. The vitals flatlined, but the camera continued to show the devastation as massive, streaking plasma rounds ripped through the atrium and pieces of debris both large and small vented into space.

"The ships," Bullock said.

"All ships move in," Condon said over the comms. "Repeat, all ships move in!"

Tarsigh and the surviving infiltrators burst onto level three. The captain stopped at the first office he came to. The wall next to the locked door was glass, and Tarsigh could see the shadow of someone crouched behind the desk. A holo on the door identified the occupant as a content coordinator. Tarsigh continued on past more offices—editors, general managers, and the like—until he came to Phil Morrow, Chief Broadcast Engineer.

Tarsigh fired a burst through the glass, rushed in, and pulled out from behind the desk a shaking, whimpering Mr. Morrow.

"Control room," Tarsigh barked in the man's ear.

"Level f-five," he answered.

Tarsigh dragged the man back out into the hall. "Level five," he said to the others.

As the captain pulled Morrow along, Sub-Captain Larabee voiced frantically in his ear: "Trouble! Big trouble. Collective . . . a whole armada. Must have been waiting behind the planet. Twelve ships."

A knot tightened in Tarsigh's stomach. Twelve ships. A hopeless situation. But the *Rapier* could still go down swinging. There had been a drone on board, which Larabee should have sent out when Tarsigh and the others launched in the *Arrow*. It had been programmed with a false identifier: not enough to stand up to close scrutiny, but enough to pass a scan.

"Maintain shields for now," he said, hauling Morrow up the stairs behind the others. "More to come."

"Copy," Larabee said.

"M-my dad was an engineer," Morrow said. "Part of the rebel underground network."

"That a fact?" Tarsigh answered.

"Yeah. Collective never found out, but I'm just sayin'—"

"You're on our side, is that it?" Tarsigh replied.

"Yes! One hundred percent."

The captain was thinking about what Striker had said when the idea of broadcasting their info about the Collective had first been brought to the table. He had said it was possible "only if they don't know we're coming."

Obviously, the Collective *did* know. They had planned an ambush at the point of entry, hidden a Collective armada behind the planet . . . what other measures had they taken against the information getting out? As they stepped onto level five, Tarsigh mused that while it was certain that Mister Morrow would say anything and everything to preserve his own life, the engineer might also prove to be their last hope against whatever contingencies still awaited them.

———•———

Bartlett put out a hand to steady himself as the lift rocked. The car was stopped on level two with its doors open. Two of his men stood just outside with guns aimed in either direction. It sounded as if the station was being blown apart.

A lens over Bartlett's left eye provided a readout from the station computer. It had recognized Tarsigh and played the video of him and the others up on level three, grabbing some employee. It then provided an image of the pirates' current location, on level five. He motioned for the two men to come back in, then reached out and hit the number five button on the lift.

"They're heading for the main control room," he shouted both into the comm and to the men in the car. Four had made it into the lift with him. Two more must have gotten into one of the other lifts. A readout on his heads-up display showed seven of his team left. His heart was beating into his throat. So far, things weren't exactly going to plan. He *could not* fail. Not again.

He spit a curse as they hit level five, the doors opened, and the first man to lean out was cut down.

Condon's fingernails dug into his palms, close to breaking skin.

He reminded himself that they had taken steps; it would be impossible for the Ridgerunners to succeed. There was no way these pirates could truly hope to take on the Collective and win.

At his side, Bullock blurted into her comm: "*Apex, Sterling*, get transports with backup out to the station, now!"

The captains' voices came back: "Yes ma'am," and "Right away."

"Flagship *Excel*," Condon said into his comm. "Drone status?"

The captain's voice came back: "No unidentified drones within our scanning radius, sir."

"Good," Condon answered. "All ships, focus fire on that single vessel."

"Hurry it up!" Tarsigh blurted.

Morrow held his wrist to a reader next to the door. There was a beep as the door slid open, granting them entry to the main control room.

The captain had handed over the disk, upon which he had copied the evidence against the Collective along with a short message. Morrow certainly appeared convinced that his life now depended on broadcasting what he had been given, as the sweaty, thin man began frantically pressing buttons and typing commands.

The Dane Koros trial, being transmitted from Earth, was being relayed through the station, playing on several monitors overhead, without sound. Other monitors displayed various programs. Another monitor just in front of them flashed and began playing both the audio and video of Tarsigh's message.

"Data's good," Morrow said.

"Transmit it!"

Morrow's hands flew to obey while in the passage outside, Tarsigh's remaining fighters continued to hold off the Collective. One of his men guarded the main entry of the control room, another covered the lift bank from this side, and the third held a position on the lift's far side. Bartlett's crew was pinned down.

That was all well and good, but Morrow looked as if he was about to pass out. "Our, uh, our transmitter's being jammed," he croaked.

So *that* was the Collective's contingency plan. "Pinpoint the source," Tarsigh responded, placing the barrel of his sling gun against the man's neck. Morrow held up a hand, went back to work at the terminal, then said, "It's one of the Collective ships outside. I—I can give you coordinates."

"You do that," the captain said. Then, to Larabee: "*Rapier*, prepare to receive coordinates for a Collective vessel. Get your drone in position and when I give the order, skip out and give that ship everything you've got."

"Copy," Larabee's haggard voice replied.

The Collective was jamming the station transmitter, but with all that was going on, they hadn't yet thought to jam comms. It was something, at least.

"Our shields are almost done," Larabee continued. "I think we'll only get one shot at this."

"Understood," Tarsigh said.

CHAPTER 24

On board the *Rapier*, Sub-Captain Larabee awaited confirmation from Spaulding, his second, that the drone was in position. The ship they would be targeting was the Collective flagship, whose identifier came back as *Excel*.

"Shields at five percent," Spaulding stated. "But the drone's ready. They've left it alone."

"Okay, this is it." All or nothing. "Skip on my mark and be ready to fire: three, two . . . one . . . mark!"

Silence hung. Larabee and the others held their breath, waiting for the view outside the observation window to change.

It didn't.

"What happened?" Larabee yelled.

"I . . . I don't know, the drone's . . . delayed. Shields at two percent . . ."

Larabee's mind thrummed: if they skipped, they could evade fire long enough to launch all ordnance on *Excel*, but once their shields were down, in their current position the missiles might not even make it out of their silos.

"Drone's still . . . struggling. Shields are—"

"Fire! Fire!"

The shields came down; the ship shuddered violently from multiple strikes.

"Tactical's gone," Spaulding yelled as the *Rapier* continued to rock. "Only half the missiles made it out . . ."

With half the missiles, *Excel* would take damage, but it wouldn't be enough.

Just then the scene outside the observation window *did* change. They were now positioned above and behind the *Excel*. Whatever had happened, it had only delayed their skip. But . . .

"Missiles?" Larabee asked.

"Nothing left," Spaulding answered.

"Plasma?"

"Depleted."

"Li," Larabee said to the navigations officer, "can you pilot us *into* her?"

"Gravity thrusters non-responsive," Li answered.

"Repair crews are working," Spaulding said.

Larabee nearly told him not to bother, but at least the engineers could feel a sense of purpose in their final moments.

The floor quaked beneath them as the ship once again began absorbing damage. A few of the Collective's armada would have caught on to the trick and relocated by now.

"*Excel* is attempting to make contact," the communications officer relayed.

Larabee shook his head and said: "Give 'em silence."

This was it, then. They had come to the end. Boarding crews would reach them in minutes. Larabee punched a button on the seat. "Captain, this is Larabee. We failed. The drone . . . something went wrong. I'm sorry."

He didn't wait for Tarsigh's response before saying to Spaulding, "Ready final measure."

Spaulding silently obeyed, initiating the ship's self-destruct sequence.

Spirion wondered if his counter tactic had worked. During the brief time he had been in possession of the data cube, and from the adaptor itself, he had gleaned just enough of an understanding of the Europan next-gen tech to write a program, which he had provided to the Collective. If his suppositions were correct, the gravity pulse carriers being sent out by the armada would interfere with the drone technology: maybe not enough to negate it fully, but at the very least he felt confident the signal would hinder it. And as long as the pulse was transmitted in all directions, they didn't even have to target the drone directly. As long as it was within range, it should be affected.

The most immediate concern, of course, was Tarsigh. Spirion had never been particularly vain, but the marring of his features was an offense that could not go unanswered.

He had hung back on purpose, not entirely trusting in the ability of Bartlett and his goons to repel the Pack's attack. And thus far, his instincts had proven correct. Far better, he had thought, to wait up on level eight and listen to the battle play out over the comms, wait for Bartlett to hash the job, and then swoop in and finish Tarsigh off. The greatest pity was that the captain had apparently undertaken this task with only the one ship. It would do for now. Spirion was content to wait for his chance at the remaining Pack members.

As Spirion rapidly descended the staircase toward level five, he smiled. For now, the greatest prize was his: Tarsigh's time had come.

CHAPTER 25

We failed. The drone . . . something went wrong. I'm
sorry."

The *Rapier* was finished. How had the drone failed?

"Copy," Tarsigh responded. He held a hand to his head
as Morrow waited, watching the data from Tarsigh's disk
where it played on the lone monitor.

A message that would not be seen outside of this room.

Tarsigh was unsure what else to say to Larabee. What
could he say that would possibly matter? "You will not be
forgotten," he managed. "What was done here today was not
done in vain. The people will wake up. The truth . . . will not
end with us."

Tarsigh waited for a response, but none came.

Morrow cast a sideways glance and Tarsigh believed he read genuine regret in the man's eyes. Just as the captain went to join his comrade at the control room entry, the ally fell to a barrage of enemy fire. Outside, the gunfire ceased.

"Remaining units, report," he said into the headpiece. Silence was the only answer.

It was over. What was left now, but to die a good death? A warrior's death.

Even as Tarsigh thought this, an arc grenade came bouncing into the room.

Tarsigh grabbed Morrow by the wrist and slung him toward the side door. He followed just behind, shoving the man to the side and clearing the doorway just as the grenade detonated.

Condon's heart raced. He was never this close to the action— never in the thick of it.

The Pack vessel had just blown itself to pieces and taken the Collective boarding party—which had just docked— with it.

On the tactical monitors, the explosion had been breathtaking.

The hovering displays relaying the individual soldier POVs showed Bartlett and his team finally getting out of the lift onto level five; they all moved at once, three of them aiming guns to either side as they set foot into the hallway and split up. After an exchange which resulted in two more of the strike team dead, the pirates on either end of the passage were finally gunned down.

The team then stacked up and moved around a corner, closing on the control room. There was only one Ridgerunner guarding it; the team made fairly short work of him. Then, one of the men tossed in a grenade.

A soldier called over: "Reinforcements have arrived at the station."

"Good," Bullock replied from a few feet away.

Condon had one hand balled into the other at his chest, eyes glued to the camera feeds. Had they done it? Was the pirate captain dead?

Tarsigh's ears rang steadily.

Morrow was seated against the wall, hands clasped over his head, chin tucked, eyes squeezed shut. He opened them, blinked, unclasped his hands, and looked around in amazement at being alive.

Tarsigh reached out to the man's jaw. He swiveled the man's face toward his own, squeezed tight, leaned in, and said loudly, "Be one of the good ones."

And then he was up and off toward the end of the small hallway. He stepped into the main corridor, unleashing a barrage of sling gun fire.

"Behind you!" Morrow shouted.

Tarsigh spun, sighting . . . Spirion. Alive, after all. The weasel had just stepped through the stairway door and had his gun raised, just inches away. Tarsigh batted the weapon out of the vermin's hand and raised his own gun, but Spirion grasped the barrel and lifted, up and over. The first bullet grazed Spirion's right thigh; successive gunfire shredded the walls and ceiling. Spirion yanked, and the gun flew from both their grips; Tarsigh head-butted the slightly taller man. Spirion stumbled back, threw a wild punch that Tarsigh blocked—and then he answered with his own, a solid hook that caught the rat-faced pirate on the jaw and sat him down.

Just behind was an open doorway; a maintenance access lay beyond some engineer's tools littering the floor—and past that, an expanse of some kind.

Sounds of movement came from the rear. No time to go for either of their guns. With a primal roar, Tarsigh rushed into Spirion just as the other man regained his feet, and propelled both of them through the short access hall and out into the void.

CHAPTER 26

As the two men fell into the open shaft, they separated. Tarsigh grasped the first thing his hands came into contact with, while Spirion continued to fall, striking something else, a robot of some kind. The captain took an instant to assess his surroundings: it seemed they were in some kind of archives. . . a repository large enough to serve as a storehouse for all of the programs the station aired. It was cylindrical in shape, with a pillar extending through the center. Storage drives lined both the mast and the inner walls. The shaft took up a great amount of space and seemed to stretch from the highest level to nearly the lowest. Robots with articulated arms and platforms for data disk storage moved about, hovering between heights, withdrawing disks and replacing them. Tarsigh had grabbed onto the arms of one robot, while Spirion had fallen onto the platform of a lower one that had been passing beneath its counterpart.

Tarsigh glanced down now to see Spirion standing on that same platform, retrieving something from a sheath on his right thigh.

It was a pressure-bladed machete.

Spirion's robot deposited a disk, then rose and passed once again under Tarsigh's. The captain tucked his legs up, knees to his chest as Spirion swiped with the machete, missing him by only the merest fraction.

Tarsigh was fully at the mercy of his robot's routines, unable to pilot the machine himself. With Spirion's technical knowledge, he wondered if his enemy might be able to, but he suspected that would take tools and a bit of time.

Tarsigh swung around so he was facing his robot's platform, his hands on either side of the arm. He kicked one leg up and then the other and haphazardly made his way onto the tray. Spirion and his robot were nowhere in sight as Tarsigh's machine ascended at a dizzying speed, past the access he had charged through, up near the very top of the shaft. He was kneeling, steadying himself. His robot withdrew a disk; he shifted as the arm placed it near his right leg.

The robot then descended rapidly; for an instant Tarsigh was weightless before the machine stopped roughly a quarter of the way from the bottom and circled around the central mast. Spirion came into view, holding his machete at the ready, favoring his left leg just slightly as, for a few tense seconds, it seemed the two machines might collide.

Spirion's robot rose; Tarsigh's fell. The treacherous pirate had the high ground. Grinning, he leapt, swinging the machete in a deadly diagonal arc.

Tarsigh stood and raised his left arm to block; the machete split through his jury-rig shoulder protection, lodging itself in the meat of his deltoid. The machine once again ascended. Tarsigh reached up and grasped Spirion's collar in a cross-grip, yanking downward, forcing the other man to lean as he brought the full force of his knee into Spirion's gut. The pirate blew a gust of air. Tarsigh hooked an arm under his opponent's left armpit, spun, kicked Spirion's left leg from under him, and heaved with all his weight.

The robot was once again near the uppermost height of the shaft. Tarsigh leapt, gained the floor of the access, and stumbled in. Tarsigh took one knee and watched over the edge as his foe's flailing body smashed into the central pillar, dislodging drives, and finally struck the floor with bone-shattering force. The machete landed an instant later, burying itself in the center of the treacherous man's chest.

As the robot ascended, Tarsigh sighted the access. If he timed his jump just right . . . Tarsigh leapt, gained the floor of the access and stumbled in. He fought to catch his breath, his left arm hanging limp and useless at his side. When he looked up, a figure blocked his path. He recognized the face: Bartlett, that was the man's name. The very same Collective captain Aladhra had convinced him to set free. A throng of Collective soldiers stood behind him.

"Well now," Bartlett said, "shall we discuss the terms of your surrender?"

Just a few feet away, Tarsigh sighted his fallen sling gun.

A good death. Strength from within.

RIDGERUNNERS

Tarsigh dove downward, and with his good hand, swept up the gun; as he raised the weapon, Bartlett fired.

CHAPTER 27

Aladhra paced the Skipjack's bridge.
The hours had passed far too slowly. No one had slept.
Aladhra pushed Braxx and his engineers to the breaking
point. And Kring . . . Kring had retired to a guest cabin on
the *Skipjack*, hopefully sleeping off a drinking binge the likes
of which Aladhra had rarely seen.

Meanwhile, the Dane Koros trial played on the far
screen. It had been a constant reminder of . . . everything.
The war, the lie that had set her against Tarsigh, the treachery
of her father, but mostly it was a reminder of what Aladhra
must now set right.

Just a few moments ago the screen had gone black, quickly

replaced with a message saying ISNN was experiencing technical difficulties.

Aladhra had waited, standing before the monitor, praying to gods that she had never believed in that Tarsigh's face would appear on the screen, that his message and the data he had copied would play for all to see.

But no message had aired. For nearly half an hour nothing had shown on the screen but the technical difficulties message. The implications of this terrified her.

She stopped at the captain's chair, hit a button. "Braxx, make final adjustments. We're leaving in five."

"Ladhi, the ship's still not—"

"It wasn't a request," she answered.

"Just received a message from Fletcher, captain of the cargo hauler," Gungan reported.

"Play it," Aladhra said.

"This is Captain Fletcher of the *Star Runner*," a thick, gruff voice announced. "I regret to inform you I cannot comply with your request regarding the additional drones."

Aladhra's hands balled into fists.

"There is a high degree of Collective military activity outside Mars," Fletcher continued. "An entire armada is present and the risk is simply too great. Please accept my sincerest apologies. My crew and I are now en route to Farpost Four. Please advise at your earliest convenience."

Aladhra kicked the captain's seat savagely. Once. Twice.

Just then audio and picture came back to the far monitor.

"This is Alicia Kimbrough, reporting from the bridge of the Collective flagship *Excel*, where news continues to unfold regarding a suspected sabotage of ISNN headquarters by a pirate contingent called the Pack. This attack temporarily halted ISNN broadcasting."

Aladhra walked to the monitor, her rage momentarily forgotten, replaced now by a sickening, growing dread. The operations crew all came to stand before the screen.

The *Excel* captain spoke of the attack, the armada's engagement, and said that one Ridgerunner ship had been destroyed.

Faces fell in response to this. Braxx stepped onto the bridge and joined the audience.

"And what about the pirates on the station itself? Do we have any estimate of casualties yet, and have the attackers been—wait," the reporter put a hand to her headpiece. "We have a live feed coming in from the station. I'm told this is a . . . Captain Bartlett. Captain, go ahead."

The image on screen was replaced by a man with short, thinning dark hair and a round face, smiling widely. Captain Bartlett, standing against a wall. Aladhra's heart clenched; her gut twisted at the sight of the man. This was the man she had fought for, him and his crew—she had convinced Tarsigh to spare them.

"I'm very happy to report that the pirates have been neutralized," Bartlett said. "Not only that but as an added bonus . . ."

Bartlett gestured to his side; the camera panned to reveal a body, staged against a medical stretcher, propped against the wall. It was Tarsigh.

Aladhra's hands flew to her mouth. There was a slug-sized hole in the center of the captain's forehead.

Bartlett came to stand next to the body. "With this victory, I feel confident that it's only a matter of time until the rest of the Pack has been tracked down and dealt with.

They'll be leaderless, in a state of despair and chaos, and the Collective will most assuredly take advantage of that."

The bridge was silent. Aladhra looked over all of their faces. Striker's head was buried in his hands. Braxx was weeping, unable to look at the monitor any longer. Jepps's jaw was clenched. Findlay stared, mouth open. Gungan had bowed his head.

Without a word, Aladhra strode off the bridge.

Condon was glad to be back on Earth once again.

The Mars operation had been—largely—a success. The Ridgerunner captain was dead, yes, but the fact that the only pirate ship present had been destroyed meant that their knowledge of the Europan space-jumping technology was still incredibly limited. And the one informant they had access to who knew at least *something* about the Europan tech was now dead. At least his countermeasure had survived, and proven to be effective in delaying the Ridgerunners' relocating abilities. That tech was even now being replicated, in the hopes of duplicating the result.

All in all, Condon wasn't nervous when he was summoned by the Old Man, whose hovering suite was now passing over Africa.

When he stepped in, the HR representative for Condon's team, Danique, was seated before Folk's desk.

This made Condon slightly nervous. The Miracle Boy himself, Old Man Folk, was hunched in his chair, head tilting slightly to the left, face slack. His eyes slowly registered

Condon's presence.

"Mm, you made it. Have a seat," Folk said hoarsely.

Condon eyed Danique warily as he crossed behind her and sat. She looked over, her face a blank canvas, then turned to face the Old Man once again.

"The Mars mission," Folk said, "how do you think that went?"

Sweat broke out on Condon's skin. Starting off with "How do you think that went?" was a tactic he used himself, and it was never, ever, a good thing. His thoughts reeled. How many of the failures could he blame on Bullock? What was his backup? Bullock had pressed him to send the ships in. Perhaps if they had waited the other Ridgerunners would have—

"Relax," the Old Man said, holding up a hand. "I'm just having some fun with you. I could see those wheels turning." He smiled. "Let me guess, you were about to throw Bullock to the wolves." Before Condon could respond Folk said, "Of course you were. That's what I taught you. And that's why you're here. I have good news for you, son . . ."

Folk had never called Condon "son."

The old man reached out a knobby finger and pushed a button on his desk. Five floating holographic screens appeared above and behind him. They displayed the faces of two men and three women: the CEOs of Collective Moon, Mars, Enceladus, Titan, and Dione.

A light shone from the desk onto Folk's face. "I'll make this quick," he said. "Some of you may have guessed this already, but due to failing health I'm stepping down as CEO of Collective Earth. Effective immediately upon my resignation, which will be official in a few days, my replacement will be the current Vice President of Special Operations and Emerging Technologies, Brenn Condon."

CHAPTER 28

Aladhra sat in her cabin, watching ISNN.

Nearly a full rotation had passed since the grim announcement and display of Tarsigh's corpse. The ship had been quiet; Braxx continued his repairs, giving intermittent updates on comms. Aladhra assumed the other ships were focusing on repairs as well. She had stayed inside her room. Instead of smashing everything in sight, as part of her desperately wanted to do, she had simply sat on her bed, knees tucked to her chest, working through things in her head and in her heart, sorting through the self-condemnation and trying to find a place where she could have any hope of carrying on, of moving ahead with some kind of purpose.

More details about the attack had been aired, the most disturbing of which was the fact that the Collective puppet, Bartlett, had been the one to put the slug through Tarsigh's skull. The boot-licker had even gotten a commendation and was once again captain of his own vessel, this time of an Earth-assigned flagship, the *Superior*.

All of which was simply more salt in Aladhra's wounds.

On the monitor, the reporter Alicia Kimbrough was interviewing a man who had been supposedly taken hostage by Tarsigh and the team from the *Rapier*. Phil Morrow was his name. "It was terrible," he said. "A whirlwind of chaos." He looked at the camera as he said this.

Aladhra frowned. A whirlwind of chaos . . . interesting. Very interesting. She would need to speak with Braxx about that.

Kimbrough wrapped up her interview and handed the broadcast over to ISNN Earth, where the final verdict in the Dane Koros trial was to be read.

This was, Aladhra knew, just a formality. There was no doubt as to what the verdict would be. The camera lingered on Koros, seated, chin up, back straight, waiting for his fate to be declared. A tight close-up then as the judge's face filled the screen.

"A verdict has been reached," he said gravely. "Dane Koros: the Collective finds you . . . guilty of sedition." Cheers erupted in the courtroom. The camera cut to Koros, stone-faced. Defiant.

"The sentence is death by hanging. To be carried out in three days. Your crimes have finally caught up to you, Mr.

Koros. You will be a plague upon the system no longer." The judge banged his gavel.

Aladhra, at last, came to a decision. "Monitor, mute," she said, then called up Braxx on comms.

"Aye, Ladhi," he answered.

"Call a meeting," she said. "All of command. Immediately."

Ten minutes later, Aladhra was seated in her usual spot at the table. Tarsigh's chair was conspicuously vacant. She was lost in her own thoughts, staring at that seat when Braxx entered and took his spot. For the moment it was just the two of them.

"There were songs that were played," she said.

Braxx looked at her confoundedly.

"During the war, there were songs that were played by sympathizers, messages to the rebel underground."

"Aye," Braxx answered.

"One of those songs was *Whirlwind of Chaos*, wasn't it?"

"It was," Braxx confirmed.

"The Collective ever catch onto that?"

"Not that I know of," the big man answered. "Why?"

"Maybe nothing," Aladhra said.

The others had begun filing in now—including Jepps, at Aladhra's request—taking their seats silently.

"Sub-captains too," Aladhra said.

Gungan took a moment to patch in the sub-captains, then gave Aladhra a nod.

Kring was the last to arrive, looking disheveled and despondent as he took a seat.

"There are some things that need to be said," Aladhra began. "That I want all of you to hear."

The team waited in silence.

"I went after Tarsigh in this very room," she continued. "Most of you saw it. A blind rage based on misinformation. Misunderstanding. That's not an excuse; it's just fact. There is no excuse for what I did. The reason Tarsigh left . . ." Aladhra's throat caught. She swallowed and kept on, "was to protect me. To protect all of us."

"I should have been on that ship!" Kring suddenly spoke up. "I should have died with my men!"

"And I heard that it was all Braxx could do to hold you back," Aladhra answered. "I'm not telling you that I have a monopoly on guilt. I don't. Tarsigh did what he did hoping to get this bounty off our heads by striking a crippling blow to the Collective. He failed; he died. For us. And now we have to figure out what our future looks like in the aftermath of that. I've been . . . more hindrance than help. My attitude . . . my anger has been misplaced. I have to live with my share of the guilt for Tarsigh's sacrifice. But before I figure out how to do that, I needed to speak to all of you."

She looked over to the empty seat. "Tarsigh left a message for me. He wanted me to be captain when he left. Like I said, I've made a lot of mistakes. But I've also learned from them. If not, I wouldn't even think about saying what I'm about to say."

The room remained quiet as Aladhra said, "I want to be your captain. Whether that happens or not is up to you. All of you. I'm putting it to a vote. If you vote in support of it, then I'll sit in that chair and I'll tell you how I plan to move forward. If you vote against, I'll leave the Pack and I'll never bother any of you again. So that's it. I'm putting it to a vote right now. This is *your* choice, not mine. All in favor. . . ?"

For a moment there was only silence, but that moment was brief. Braxx spoke first. "Aye," he said. Striker was next, then Findlay, Gungan, Jepps . . . Kring hesitated the longest, but answered in the affirmative. Then, one by one, the sub-captains' voices came through the comm. The vote was unanimous.

Aladhra nodded, rose from her seat, and settled herself into Tarsigh's chair. She squeezed its arms until her knuckles turned white, then said, "My first act as captain . . ." She nodded to Kring. "Kring, the post of Second is open. I want that to be you. Do you accept?"

Kring looked around. "Me, why?" he asked.

"Because I'm very aware of what your crew thought of you. You're a natural leader."

And because he needed a crew to replace the one he lost, she thought.

Kring took a long moment to consider, and finally nodded. "It would be my honor."

"Come sit next to me."

Kring got up, came and took the seat Aladhra had just vacated.

"Okay," she said. "Striker, you're going to pull a file from the data cube after this meeting. There's something on there, something specific, that Tarsigh said could 'chop the head off the snake.'" Her eyes traveled around the table. "We're also going to get our drones back from *Star Runner*. This is how we're going to move forward, and this is how I'm going to come to terms with my own failings: we're going to take the piece of information Tarsigh described and we're going to present it for all to see, at an event that will be aired to the entire system: at the same time we do that, we're going to save a comrade who has been unjustly condemned to death."

Aladhra leaned forward. "In three rotations, we're going to rescue Dane Koros."

CHAPTER 29

Aladhra had never been religious. Most of the Pack weren't. They believed that human beings forged their own destinies, created their own opportunities, and in many cases, brought about their own consequences in the case of wrongdoing. They didn't look to some deity to guide their fortunes, and they didn't look to salvation in an afterlife. When one of their own died, they said a few words, they shared stories, and they drank, and later, they fought in memory of their fallen comrade.

The funeral service for Gordo was a no-frills affair. He was laid to rest in a coffin that would fit in the tube used to launch "buster" missiles, on board his ship the *Monolith*.

Aladhra, along with the rest of the command crew, had brought the body aboard and had gathered now for the commemoration.

Takashi, the replacement captain, spoke of Gordo's intellect and natural leadership ability. Takashi said that "for a man of slight stature, he cast an immense shadow." Other members of the *Monolith* command crew spoke as well, recalling Gordo's mixture of kindness and firmness and illustrating examples of his keen capacity for problem solving. When they had finished, Aladhra spoke up.

"I didn't know Gordo nearly as well as all of you," she began. "But it's clear from what's been said here that you all respected and admired him. Based on what I knew of Gordo, I certainly share in those opinions. Above all, I'll remember his bravery and fearlessness at a time when those qualities counted most. I want us to take this time to remember the others who recently gave their lives as well; not to take away from this time dedicated to Gordo, but to put him in the exalted company of those who put their necks on the chopping block so that we can stand here and be the ones doing the remembering. Let us remember all the men and women who died; let us remember especially the crew of the *Rapier*."

At this, Kring's jaw clenched, his face contorted in an effort to hold back the emotions that seemed ready to gush forth.

"And let us remember . . ." Aladhra paused, unsure that she would get the name out without her voice breaking, "Tarsigh."

Heads nodded solemnly all around.

"Time now that we say farewell and send Gordo on his

final voyage."

Gordo's coffin glided along the loading deck into the tube, as the gathered held fists over their hearts. The breach closed, and the coffin was fired off into the endless void.

Aladhra stayed for drinks after the ceremony, along with the others. When the opportunity presented itself, she pulled Striker aside.

"Have you been studying the skip tech?" she asked.

"Exhaustively," Striker replied, then downed the entirety of his wine mug.

Aladhra had, at this juncture, elected to stop drinking.

"Good," she said. "I have some tasks for you. I want you to take the Europan material and lace it into a few different things. Also, do you still have the contact on Titan, the one who puts together false IDs?"

"Yeah," Striker said. "She's solid. *Completely* solid," he added, remembering the debacle with Garth. "So, you're finally gettin' chipped?" he asked.

Anyone under the purview of the Collective received an *ID* chip in their wrist at age twelve to replace the cards issued them at birth. Having not been born into and not growing up in the Collective's system, Aladhra had never been chipped.

"Yeah," she said. "But not just me. Get a new one for yourself. I'll give you details. And we're going to need transport. From Titan or Enceladus, whichever's easier." She leaned in and responded to Striker's questioning glance: "You and I are going to Earth ahead of the others."

———•———

Condon's mind was abuzz. There was so much to be done, preparation for the transition. Deep down he had always known this day would come. He deserved this. He had earned it. He had fought for it. All of his preparation, his determination, his unyielding, single-minded focus had led him to the *Pinnacle* of his career.

He hadn't even pursued his investigation into Bullock any further. There was no need. Once he was CEO, all of the departments' projects would be known to him, top secret or otherwise. And if Bullock was working outside the company aegis, he had no problem terminating her.

In the meantime, Condon had more pleasant things to think about. The Old Man had invited him to his New York penthouse suite to celebrate. The tube had brought Condon from L.A. in five minutes. His wrist chip had gained him automatic access to the penthouse from the lift, and he had arrived to find the door open. Together, Condon knew, the suite's various rooms allowed a 360 degree view of New Times Square. Condon had heard rumors, but he had never been here. It was, as expected, luxurious to the extreme.

He had brought with him a bottle of the system's finest merlot, which he cradled in his arm as he moved through the large, open, lavishly decorated rooms, calling for Folk. Classical music played from hidden speakers. Priceless works of art hung from every wall.

The lights dimmed as Condon made his way deeper, coming finally to the massive dining room. A thick wooden table took up nearly the entire length of the room, bounded by high-backed chairs. It was not yet set for dinner. Standing just past the end of the table was Danique. She stood perfectly still, favoring Condon with her disquieting stare.

"What . . . are you doing here?" Condon asked.

A chair with its back facing him scooted out, and a figure stood and stepped into view. Bullock allowed herself the slightest smile. "Thanks for joining us," she said.

"Where's Folk?" Condon demanded. "What have you done with him?"

"This will go a lot easier if you just relax," Bullock said.

Security. He needed to get security. They could sort out whatever had happened.

He turned and hurried from the dining room back into the chamber he had entered through, an art gallery. Old double doors to his right burst open and Danique was there, chin down, moving impossibly fast. She was on him before he could make it more than a few more steps, grasping him by the collar. He tried to punch her, but the sleeve of his suit was immediately caught up in her steel grip. Condon had an idea of what this woman was capable of; but even he didn't know the full extent of her enhancements.

With a savage grunt he swung the wine bottle up and into her temple; her head bobbed to one side from the impact, but her stare never wavered. Condon scooted backward, ducked his head, pulled back his arm, and withdrew himself from his coat.

He burst into a full run then, sprinting through the rooms in a blind frenzy. When he came at last to the foyer, the Old Man was sitting just before the ceiling-high doors, which were now closed. He was in a hover-chair, looking just as weathered as ever.

Condon came skidding to a halt just a meter away.

"The chair isn't a necessity," Folk said, "not yet, anyway.

Just makes it easier for me to get around at the end of a long day."

"I want to know what's going on," Condon said, glancing quickly behind him. "I thought they had done something to you."

"No, no," the Miracle Boy replied. "They're trying to do something *for* me. They're providing assistance. *You're* going to provide assistance as well. The process is still in its infancy and therefore still somewhat invasive. Certainly not something you'd have volunteered for, had I asked."

Condon thought instantly of Bullock. "Is this about Bullock?" He asked in a quiet, defeated voice. "Something to do with my brain?"

"Your brain's not exactly what I'm looking for," Folk answered, his tired eyes suddenly lighting up. "But Bullock . . . yes, Bullock's team has made great strides. You'll be a part of something unprecedented. We're all parts in a machine, as you know. And when a part gets too old, you replace it, don't you? Now, there'll be quite a sting," he said. "I could have drugged your food or your drink, but I was curious, you see . . ."

Condon felt a sharp, piercing pain at the back of his skull as the Old Man leaned in, grinning widely. "I've never seen you scared."

203

CHAPTER 30

Aladhra stood before the door to Sub-Captain Bloom's cell, with Braxx at her left shoulder.

The door's motor engaged, slid aside. Bloom was sitting, quiet, morose. He swallowed as Aladhra and Braxx strode in.

"I've been dealing with a lot of anger throughout my life," Aladhra said. "My subconscious has spent quite a while trying to figure out how to channel it, or simply channeling it in the wrong directions. Most recently what's brought my blood to a boil is the death of Tarsigh."

Bloom's face fell. He looked away.

"Sub-Captain Kring lost his entire crew aboard the *Rapier.* Because of you, specifically. So as you can imagine,

Kring is dealing with a fair bit of rage also." She turned to Braxx. "How many times did he threaten to bust in here and kill Bloom?"

"Several," Braxx answered.

Aladhra came and stood close to the sub-captain. "One of the things Tarsigh and I used to argue about was where to draw the line when it came to violence and death. Quite often, I argued for the benefit of the doubt, for lives to be spared. But after what you've done . . . all you are right now is a waste of this ship's oxygen. I debated letting Kring come in here and have his way. But the Pack, we live and die by a code. It's very simple but it's very specific: you betray your own, you get locked out."

Bloom moaned softly, eyes downcast.

Fifteen minutes later, Bloom was brought to the *Skipjack's* primary airlock, where the command crew had gathered. Kring, in a jury rig pressure suit, led Bloom, in his under-alls, into the chamber.

Aladhra watched through a window in the door.

Bloom was just on the other side, leaning in, his breath fogging the glass as he spoke. "I'm sorry about Tarsigh. I mean that. And about the *Rapier* . . . will you believe that, at least? Will you believe that I'm sorry? I'm not a monster."

Aladhra's eyes stayed locked on the man, silence her only answer.

Braxx stood on her right side. She turned to him, nodded, and said, "Drain it." He complied, hitting the button to depressurize the chamber.

As the air was slowly removed, Bloom turned away from the window and attacked Kring, swinging his fists wildly. Kring blocked his blows and threw a straight punch that sent Bloom stumbling back into the bulkhead. Bloom came back, slower this time, clawing at Kring's suit, with no hope of tearing through the fabric or removing the helmet. His exertions slowed further; veins all along his body stood out; his eyes bulged and his body fought to take in more oxygen, but there was none to be had. Vessels in Bloom's eyes burst; his face contorted as his muscles seized, and at last he fell heavily to the chamber floor.

A green light flashed next to the inner door to signal that the lock had been fully depleted of air. Kring looked to the window and gave a nod. Aladhra conveyed the permission to Braxx, who hit the button to open the outer door.

With the chamber depressurized, nothing within was vented into space, nor was the gravity inside affected. Kring dragged Bloom to the edge of the airlock, then came around and heaved; the body tumbled out and then hovered as if held aloft by an invisible updraft.

Kring stood watching for a moment. Behind him, through the window, Aladhra watched also as Bloom's corpse slowly floated away. It wasn't closure, not even close. But it was a step in the right direction.

She felt a tap on her shoulder and turned to see Striker, who pulled her aside.

"Sorry I missed this, but a couple things: first, I heard back about the *ID*s. We're all set for a meet in five hours. But second, a message was relayed to us, through some old back-channels. It's from that guy who was at the station when . . . when the attack happened."

Aladhra's eyes narrowed. "The one they interviewed?" she asked.

"Yeah, he wants to meet a member of the Pack at Enceladus.

Said he's there now. Has to be a trap, so I figured we'd ignore it, but—"

"He sent a message," Aladhra said, considering. "In that interview. He used an old rebel code. A song title. I'll meet him."

"I don't think that's—"

"We'll be smart about it," Aladhra said. "Do it on our terms. But I want to hear what he has to say."

Phil Morrow's heart threatened to beat its way right out of his chest.

For the thousandth time, he weighed the notion of simply leaving. Traveling to Enceladus had been expensive, and he was going to meet *Ridgerunners*, for God's sake. Criminals. Pirates. Then he weighed the other reasons to do what he was doing and once again, those justifications prevailed.

He had received a message through the same back-channel he had used to make contact, telling him that a cruiser had been rented in his name at a low-level tour-operation and travel agency in orbit around Enceladus.

He chipped in at the desk, went to the berth, through the airlock and into the rented cruiser. Coordinates had been preprogrammed into the vessel. He guided the ship out of the bay and let autopilot take him, wondering what was in store. The precautions were not surprising, given the Pack's situation. More than anything, Morrow just hoped that their new captain would hear him out.

By the time he reached the designated location, the small ship had exceeded its recommended travel range. The coordinates had led him to, as far as he could tell, empty space. He asked the computer to perform a systems check, just to pass the time. Halfway through, the vessel's low-grade scanners picked up an arriving vessel, announcing the discovery with a pleasant pinging noise. This sound was followed by another. And another. And another . . .

Soon, Morrow's tiny ship was surrounded.

A female voice came through the speakers, stating, "Engage docking protocols. Then stay in your seat and prepare to be boarded."

Morrow did as he was told. The cruiser docked with a sigma-class Ridgerunner vessel. With the pilot's chair spun around, Morrow watched and waited. Moments later a young woman came through the airlock, accompanied by an incredibly large and intimidating man with long hair, a beard, and a tattoo on his cheek. As for the woman, Morrow assumed immediately by the way she carried herself and the way her eyes bored into him that her attractiveness was matched by her ability to beat him senseless.

She eased into a passenger seat across from him. The man stood, watching carefully, and Morrow felt himself shrinking under his glare.

"Why did you want to meet?" the woman asked.

"Uh . . . my name's Phil. Morrow. My dad was part of the rebel—"

"Why are we here?" she pressed. The tattooed man remained quiet.

Morrow forced his nervously wringing hands onto his lap. "Right. The man who was your captain, according to the reports. Tarsigh?"

"What about him?"

"Well, he saved my life."

The woman relaxed a bit. Morrow proceeded to recount the circumstances of the attack, the grenade that nearly obliterated him, and the captain's actions, ending with his parting words to Morrow, to "be one of the good ones."

"And then he was attacked," Morrow said. "By another Ridgerunner."

The woman leaned in. The man frowned. Morrow said, "I overheard his name: Spirion."

It was a name that was clearly known to the two of them. The woman's lips parted; her eyes strayed in consideration. The man's fists clenched.

"But your captain, he won," Morrow added quickly. "It wasn't Spirion who killed Tarsigh, as you may have heard in the reports. Your captain, in fact, succeeded in killing Spirion."

The woman nodded, smiling just the slightest bit, her eyes wetly reflecting the overhead lights. The man lifted his chin proudly.

"I saw just a bit of what was on that disk," Morrow said. "You hear rumors, sometimes, about what the Collective does, but . . . I didn't really know. No one does except the higher-ups, I guess. I just . . . I reached out to you because I know something that could help you. I heard things during the investigation, and I did a little bit of digging on my own. That ship of yours that blew itself up—I pieced together that it was supposed to be able to escape. Relocate itself. But that failed or was at least delayed by a measure the Collective used."

The woman was leaning forward now, listening intently.

"They used a pulsed gravity carrier. I don't know specifics, but I believe it was this that interrupted whatever your Pack ship was supposed to do. My understanding is that this countermeasure was contributed by Spirion."

The woman and the man exchanged a look.

"He won't be providing them with any more help, at least," Morrow concluded.

The corner of the woman's mouth lifted just slightly.

Morrow let out a long breath, a bit more convinced that he might make it through this meeting in one piece.

CHAPTER 31

When Condon awoke, he was seeing and hearing through a fog. Bullock's face hovered over his, mouthing words that he couldn't readily interpret. Another face, that of a stranger, joined hers. The stranger's clothing suggested that she was a doctor.

Bullock looked to the doctor, nodded, and a headpiece came into view. Condon tried to move, to yell out for help, but his body wouldn't respond as the headpiece was fastened on. A jolt of pain from one side of his skull to the other made him squeeze his eyes shut.

The pain eased somewhat as a long procession of thoughts and memories filed through his mind's eye. It began with the

Old Man in the hover-chair and Danique attacking him at Folk's penthouse and from there it continued, memory by memory—the announcement of his promotion, the attack at ISNN, the surreptitious use of the sit-in droid, the visit to MARSA, his first meeting with Bullock, his unceremonious split with one girlfriend after another, his promotion to vice president, his graduation from college, his years in the private academy, his first kiss, getting chipped, his first steps, and on and on, rewinding the years: every breakfast, lunch, and dinner; every visit to the gym; every dream and nightmare he remembered upon awakening; every experience, the sum total of which comprised the identity that was Brenn Condon.

And then there was a sense of . . . disconnectedness. Similar to what he thought it might be like in a sensory deprivation chamber. There was just him, and the void around him. And in this state he remained, as time became inconsequential.

Aladhra was a reporter. At least that was what her false *ID* claimed. Her hair was once again styled to resemble that of all the other sheep in the system. But even more ridiculous was the makeup and business suit she was forced to wear.

Striker was her cameraman. The two of them sat with their backs to the bulkhead of a beta-class transport vessel en route to Earth. As terrible as Aladhra felt she looked, she could at least find solace in the fact that Striker looked even more ridiculous. Where he normally had stubble, he was now clean shaven, and his long hair had been gelled and pulled back into a tail.

Aladhra mentally reviewed her plan for the one hundredth time. "Be safe and be smart," Tarsigh had advised in his video to her. There was, of course, no guarantee of safety for a mission that would take them so deep behind enemy lines. But . . . Aladhra believed that she was being smart. Every stage of the operation had been carefully thought through. If it worked, not only would they liberate Dane Koros, but they would deal a blow right to the heart of the Collective. The nagging doubt that consumed her now was simply this: had she considered all of the variables carefully enough?

Before leaving, Striker had performed a series of tests on the new objects they had integrated the Europan material into. Those tests had been successful. Striker had also programmed the drones to detect and cancel out the Collective's pulsed gravity carrier using an inverted signal.

But several variables still existed: Morrow could have been lying, or if Striker made even the slightest mistake in his modifications, their drones might still be affected by the Collective response, either of which could end in death for the two of them—for they had both vowed not to be taken alive—and death or potential capture for the others. She had to trust in her team, trust in the plan. Most important of all, she had to trust in herself.

That was one thing her father had tried early on to instill in her: confidence, self-assurance. Her father . . . recently, the more she thought of him, the more he seemed like a stranger. She had sifted through memories, things he had said, tried to piece together clues that he may have provided—unwittingly or otherwise—as to his duplicity. There was nothing overt that she could remember. Just the slightest intuition on her part. Even at that young age.

She wondered how things might have been different, had her mother been alive during the time of the rebellion. Would she have been a traitor, too? Or would she have exercised an influence over Cole that would have guided him away from treachery? Aladhra chided herself for asking questions that would never be answered.

"Get ready," Striker said next to her, drawing her from her reverie. "Checkpoint."

They had arrived at Earth Sentry Station Four, where their transport had docked to allow Collective agents to board and process the ship.

Two uniformed sentries made their way, passenger by passenger, using chip readers to verify identity. Striker held up his wrist to the agent on their side. "Damron . . . Musk," the agent read off of his device. "What do you do, Damron?"

"Cameraman, sir," Striker replied. The agent eyed the lensed orb hovering above, at the sentry's eye level. He pulled a scanner from his belt and ran it over the sphere while Aladhra and Striker waited silently. Satisfied that it hid no explosives or armament, he moved on to Aladhra. He ran the reader over her wrist, pausing briefly. He remained silent, eyeing the readout. Then he leveled a deep, penetrating stare at her. Had Striker's contact botched the ID? Was this the variable that would undo the mission before it had even begun?

She told herself to keep calm.

"Tamara Kline?" he finally said.

"That's me," Aladhra said, offering her sweetest smile.

The agent continued staring. In her peripheral vision she

saw Striker shifting in his seat. She wanted to yell at him not to blow it, but she remained silent, holding the smile that was now beginning to strain her face muscles.

Finally the agent smiled back, wagging a finger at her. "I think I saw one of your broadcasts last cycle when I visited Titan."

She felt her face relax. "I get that a lot," she said.

"Well, it's gonna be a great day," the agent said. "I can't wait to see that pirate swing."

Aladhra offered another smile, though it was strained. "It'll be a day to remember," she said.

As they were led past to the outer checkpoint, Aladhra attached her headpiece and tried to recall everything she had learned about the Performance Center.

It occupied thirty hectares of land in Washington, D.C. Victory Arch, nearly twice as tall as the Washington Monument at three hundred and twenty meters, dominated the northernmost quadrant. The Arch had been built to commemorate the Collective's triumph over the rebellion, and it was here, from the Arch's crown, that seditionists were hung for all to see. Execution events were broadcast live and relayed throughout the system.

Aladhra observed her surroundings carefully as she and Striker were led past the main gate. The land's periphery was hemmed by a fifteen-meter-high wall. A single autonomous R-5 Regulator mech outfitted with a plasma gatling arm stood guard at the gate, along with a lightly armored contingent of peacekeepers.

The atmosphere on the grounds and in the tiered seating was, for the most part, one of jubilation. Vendors sold refreshments, the latest chart-toppers blasted over hovering speakers, and holotrons splashed selected content on mammoth screens. Patrolling peacekeeper autocars hovered throughout.

Aladhra had never been to Earth. Gravity drives on ships and stations throughout the system were based on Earth gravity, so the planet's pull didn't feel any different to her. But Striker had warned her about the brightness of the sun, and she was glad for the shade-lenses he'd suggested she wear as they were taken to the reserved media station on a raised section at the foot of the Arch.

Looking up, they could see the large platform that stretched from one side of the arch's upper section to the other. A long cable hung from the peak, ending in a noose just two meters from the platform surface, where a small knot of Collective Guard and the master of ceremonies currently stood.

The emcee was a short, middle-aged man whom Aladhra vaguely recognized as a popular talk show host. Manny Spangler was the name, if she remembered correctly.

He held out his hands to start the show. "Welcome, good citizens of Earth, and welcome to all of you watching throughout the system! The great boss man himself could not be here, busy as he is overseeing all the moving parts that make up the Collective. But! He did record a message for this auspicious occasion. You all know who I'm talking about . . . the Miracle Boy himself, the CEO of Collective Earth, Pindl Folk!"

The crowd voiced its appreciation. "Direct your attention to the holotrons!"

Pindl Folk's image dominated over half of the massive screens. The remaining holographic planes depicted camera footage of not just the cheering crowd at Performance Center, but they cut between wide-angle views of similar crowds gathered at places on the moon, Mars, Enceladus, Titan, and Dione.

The Old Man was truly liked, nearly revered, Aladhra mused. He provided a face, a mask of humanity on what was in fact just a grinding, soulless, relentless machine. Folk looked haggard, gaunt, a few steps away from death, but his eyes gleamed. "Today is a great day!" he rasped. "Today a balance will be struck! Today a crippling liability will be eliminated!" The Old Man shook and coughed violently before regaining composure. "Today, our entire system will profit from the meaningful contributions of its heroic protectors! This success will be richly rewarded! And now *you* will all be rewarded, with the opportunity to witness the price our enemies pay for failure! I only wish I could be there to share in the momentous experience. Just know that I'm with you all in spirit. Alright then, enough of my rambling. Return your attention to the arch, and enjoy the show!"

Folk's face winked out, replaced by a closeup of the platform where a facility transport swooped in and eased, side-on, to the back. The crowd waited anxiously on the remaining screens.

Manny addressed the people once again: "And now we come to it, what you've all been waiting to see! The time for justice is upon us!"

The vehicle's side gate opened, and two guards escorted

Dane Koros out.

Many among the crowd cheered. Aladhra reminded herself not to hate them. They believed the lies they had been fed: that the man about to die was evil, through and through. While the emcee continued, Striker removed the lens and outer shell from the "camera," then asked a few gathered reporters to stand aside as the drone floated to a patch of open space.

"Dane Koros, you have been charged with sedition and found guilty," Manny exulted. "The time has come for you to meet the same fate as all enemies of humanity . . ."

Aladhra eyed the time on the nearest holotron. The spectacle was moving along according to schedule. She stepped to the side and waved at the nearest autocar. The vehicle angled downward and descended until it hovered just above the ground. Its side door slid open, and the peacekeeper seated within asked Aladhra what the trouble was.

"There's going to be an attack," she said.

Above, on the platform, the noose was being fitted around a struggling Dane Koros's neck.

"Yeah? How would you know that?" the peacekeeper asked.

"Because I'm one of the attackers," she said, disengaging his safety belt and yanking him from the car.

CHAPTER 32

With a few swift motions, Aladhra had retrieved the peacekeeper's sidearm and shot him in the leg. These uniformed men and women were municipal law enforcement and crowd control, people just doing their job. She wanted to avoid killing them as long as possible. She was also fully aware that sparing all of their lives was not likely to be an option.

There were screams, not far away. Several people ran for cover while a dark field of energy expanded from the drone Striker had released, taking on a cube shape, three meters to a side. The nearest reporters sought cover as well, while their cameramen recorded all that was happening.

"Do it! Do it! String him!" Manny's frantic voice shouted, his voice blaring through the speakers.

Aladhra glanced to the arch. Within its crown, a motor engaged. The cable grew taut and hoisted a kicking Dane Koros higher into the air.

On the media station floor, the drone was now gone; there was a popping sound followed by a slight rush of air as the box-shaped energy field was replaced by one of the *Skipjack's* massive transport crates. Striker opened the container door to reveal Braxx, fully armored in the Vulcan suit. Next to Braxx was a jury-rig-armored Kring—holding a sling gun in one hand and the repulsor gun in the other—and hovering around them were four drones, preprogrammed with false identifiers.

Aladhra couldn't help but be relieved that the drone swap had worked. She hoped that meant Striker's fixes had defeated the Collective countermeasure, but it was possible the Collective just hadn't activated it yet or were out of range. She tried not to think what that would mean for her crew. The drones shot away from the Ridgerunners; three of them hurtled upward at blinding speed to escape the atmosphere. Kring tossed his sling gun to Striker, then retrieved another from the container. Braxx aimed his tri-barrel at the nearest autocar, unleashing a hail of gunfire that brought it crashing to the ground.

All around them now, spectators were screaming and running.

Aladhra hurried to Braxx's side. Though she couldn't target the cable from here, at least Koros had his hands on the noose, relieving some of the pressure. He wouldn't last long, but they would all be dead if they didn't deal with the largest problem.

"We've got a mech incoming," she said to Braxx. "You'll need high ground."

"Aye," he voiced through the external speakers and was off.

Collective guards fired from the platform. Kring activated the repulsor gun's shield, which fanned out in a seven-meter radius. Kring's arm shook violently from several railgun impacts as Aladhra dove for cover behind the repulsor barrier's edge. She glanced at Striker, who was using his datapad to send the remaining drone off toward the base of the arch where it would be difficult to target. He then nodded to Aladhra and hurried away toward the eastern edge of the media station, the ground erupting just inches behind him from railgun slug impacts.

Floating stairs at the station led to a media control room. Once the tech made it there safely, Aladhra tapped Kring on the shoulder and jerked her head toward the autocar. She jumped over the wounded, writhing peacekeeper and got in. Kring braced against railgun fire and engaged the shaded visor on his helmet as he made his way around the vehicle's front.

"Hurry!" Aladhra yelled as he deactivated the shield and took a seat next to her.

A railgun slug tore through the roof and center console as she took up the controls and gunned the engine.

It had been quite a while since she had piloted an autocar, taking joyrides in one acquired by the Pack on board the *Monolith*. She had crashed that one in the docking bay. As she flew the vehicle up and under the platform, Kring held on tight to the inside handle, clearly worried she would repeat that disaster. Aladhra angled her side slightly upward and managed to urge the car higher, thrusting her arm through the open door and firing with the peacekeeper's gun on the Collective Guards, dislodging them from the platform as their transport disengaged and dove out of sight. She then fired a shot that severed the cable and sent Koros plummeting to the stage.

Issuing a sixty-second hold command to the autopilot, she leapt to the surface, followed quickly by Kring.

While Kring laid down suppressive fire on the one remaining autocar, Aladhra worked the noose off of Koros's neck. The man's face was puffy and had turned a purplish blue. He coughed violently and fought for breath. "You okay?" Aladhra asked. Koros rubbed his neck and nodded.

Aladhra scanned for immediate threats. The autocar she and Kring had exited descended to land on open ground as the Collective transport returned to the platform's west side, gate open, providing egress for five more guards. Aladhra spit a curse as they bustled through a passageway in the arch wall.

Kring hurried in front of Aladhra and Koros and activated the repulsor gun's shield, recoiling from the barrage of railgun fire. He launched the projectile, which carried the barrier with it, flying across the platform and into the guards, gathering them and plowing them back through the arch access and into the transport; the vehicle careened, and the guards, having reached the platform's edge, plummeted to their deaths.

Aladhra looked to the media control room, where screaming workers scurried out. "Striker, status," she enquired.

Even as she said this, the single drone that had been left

223

at the arch's base flew upward to a position just behind the platform. "Working," the tech officer's voice replied in her ear. She looked over to see the repulsor gun disk fly back to the barrel held out by Kring.

Koros stood up, still rubbing his neck, his complexion now much closer to normal. "You . . . shouldn't have risked yourselves," he rasped.

Aladhra offered no immediate reply as she continued assessing the situation: Kring had dispatched the autocar he had targeted, and Braxx had done a good job of shredding others; aside from the car she and Kring had used, nothing remained of the rest but smoking ruin. Looking to the main gate, she noted that nearly all of the spectators had evacuated the tiered seating. Braxx, however, had his hands full with the R-5 Regulator mech. He was backed up along the middle tier as a withering storm of plasma fire from the mech's gatling arm ripped apart the quickcrete at the structure's edge. Aladhra felt helpless. There was nothing she, Striker, or Kring could do against the mech. Not yet.

"Braxx, hold on, just hold on," she said, hoping he could hear her over the tactical channel. She looked behind her at the floating sphere.

Come on, she thought . . .

"That's not good," she heard Kring say. She turned back, alarmed to see that the mech had given up on trying to dispatch Braxx and now swung its plasma gatling arm in their direction.

———•———

Captain Bartlett's career trajectory was trending upward, as the suits would say.

He had, after all, been once again promoted to captain of a vessel, this time of the Earth Collective ship *Superior*. The flagship had been assigned patrol duty during the Dane Koros execution.

There were six ships total in the armada. More than enough to handle anything that might come their way. Which, Bartlett was convinced, would be nothing.

Until the first emergency calls came in over the comms.

Saboteurs had attacked the ceremony. Guards had been dispatched relatively quickly. At least there was an R-5 Regulator Mech on site.

"What are my orders?" Bartlett asked.

"Get a ship with countermeasures in range of the park. Hold position and prepare for possible arrival of hostiles."

"Copy that, Collective Command."

Time now to employ the counter tech that had been programmed into the armada's computers. Bartlett punched a button on his seat arm. "*Synergy*, this is *Superior*. Move into countermeasure range of the Performance Center. Maintain position there and await further commands."

"Aye, sir," came the reply. Bartlett turned to his chief mate. "I want an immediate scan of all nearby drones."

"Scanning . . ." the chief mate responded. Then: "All drones come back with identifiers," he reported.

"Cross-reference with traffic control. Put each one under a microscope until you find the fakes."

"Sir."

Bartlett leaned back in his chair. This was, as he saw

it, an opportunity. If the rest of the Pack did arrive, and he were to be the commander that put an end to them once and for all, well, there was no telling how high he could climb. He would be looking at a promotion to admiral at the very least. And from there . . . who knew? A smile crept across the captain's face.

Let them come.

CHAPTER 33

Braxx was not about to let this oversized sentry bot put Aladhra in its crosshairs.

As soon as the mech moved its gatling arm away, he took advantage, charging and then leaping from what remained of the crumbling tier's edge onto the Regulator's shoulder. He maintained a grasp with the suit's left hand, then aimed his tri-barrel gun down at the joint where the regulator's left shoulder joined the upper torso and fired a full volley; the gatling arm dropped, then separated completely and crashed to the ground. The R-5 used its remaining good arm, a grappler, to reach up, grasp the Vulcan's legs, and yank.

The Vulcan suit slammed to the earth hard enough to

create a small crater. Braxx rotated the Vulcan helmet just in time to see the mech's massive foot rise. It came crashing down, causing a massive jolt to his body as the heads-up display inside the suit went dark. Braxx attempted to move, with no result. Through the visor he observed the gargantuan limb poised to stomp down once again. There was no way for him to evade what would most certainly be a killing blow, and there were no allies close enough to intervene. Braxx howled in defiance as the foot descended.

Aladhra glanced back at the drone again, heart racing. Her head whipped back to where Braxx lay, the Vulcan armor all but destroyed, the Mech foot set to plunge downward. "NO!" she shouted, sure that she was about to witness the last seconds of Braxx's life.

Just then a loud POP! sounded from behind her. A blinding torrent of plasma fire ripped through the air just over her head, tearing into the metal goliath and reducing its bulk to little more than scattered pieces.

"Braxx, are you there?" Aladhra asked, staring at the broken armor. "Braxx, answer me!"

Then, finally, his voice came over the comms: "Aye, Ladhi. But if we make it outta this, I'll be building myself some new Vulcan armor."

Aladhra exhaled a massive sigh of relief. That relief, however, quickly turned to worry: the *Skipjack* had nearly arrived too late.

Koros had crouched when the plasma fire had streamed

over their heads. He was looking back now, as was Kring. Aladhra turned to see the ship, which had materialized from the drone Striker had piloted there. It had arrived just in time to obliterate the Regulator, but it had been delayed. "Striker," she said into her headpiece.

"I know, I know," he replied. "I'm on it, just need a tick." The delay meant that Striker's answer to the Collective countermeasure had failed. If he couldn't figure out the mistake, there might be no escape for any of them.

She cast her eyes over the grounds, satisfied that at least for the moment there was no immediate threat to the rescue party.

A voice spoke in her ear: "Captain, this is Jepps, friendly transport incoming."

The transport arrived, and hovered with the ramp lowered. Aladhra looked to Koros and said, "Go. I'll join you shortly." She hoped that was true. Either way, the *Skipjack* had explicit orders to withdraw if overwhelming reinforcements arrived, whether she was on board or not.

"I'm not leaving you behind," Koros said. "Not after—"

"Look, I just went to a lot of trouble for your rescue. Don't make me shoot you."

Koros hesitated, clearly unsure whether or not to take her seriously. Finally, he said, "Fair enough," and boarded the cruiser.

The ramp raised, and the vessel returned to *Skipjack* as Striker said in her ear: "I think I have it! I hashed something in the drones' detection protocol. I'd been so focused on the inverted signal . . ."

"Is the problem solved or not?" Aladhra demanded.

"I, uh . . . think so. I hope so."

"Me too, or we're all dead," she answered.

"If there is to be a sacrifice, let's make sure it's not for nothing," the tech officer replied.

Suddenly, Aladhra's face filled half of the holotrons. Striker had redirected them to focus on her. The other half still showed crowd reactions from the moon, Enceladus, Mars, Titan, and Dione. People had their hands over their mouths or on top of their heads, eyes wide as they still processed the battle that had taken place and been relayed across the system.

Aladhra took a deep breath. This was it, then. Time to chop the snake's head off.

She began her speech. "The man you all placed your trust in, the man you paid so much devotion to, is not who you think he is," she said. "Your so-called Miracle Boy is a fraud, and worse."

CHAPTER 34

I believe I've identified one of the false drones," Captain Bartlett's chief mate said. "It's . . . closest to the Pinnacle. Bearing 320.75."

Bartlett hit a button on the seat arm: "*Pinnacle,* this is *Superior.* We're sending coordinates for a drone now. I want you to target it and—"

Captain Bartlett's second mate spoke up: "Unidentified vessel just . . . appeared, sir. Sigma class. Fusion drive. Shields active. Bearing 320. 75."

"I'm no longer reading the drone," the chief mate said.

So, they were here. Their arrival would have been delayed by the countermeasure, but they had arrived nonetheless.

Now what remained was to exterminate them before they could make good an escape.

He called to his communications officer to be put on the tactical channel. "All ships, code red. Repeat, code red all ships. Engage the enemy and be ready for—"

"Two more, sir," the second mate reported. "Both Delta class, fusion drive, shields active. They're maneuvering. Surrounding the *Pinnacle*."

Bartlett had pulled up his holo-display, but he could also see through the observation window as the second mate continued, "Weapons active, all enemy ships."

"Ready all weapons and move to engage."

"Moving to engage. Weapons ready, aye."

All three Ridgerunner ships released missiles at once; the *Pinnacle* flew apart amid explosions, venting gases, and scattering debris.

"We've lost *Pinnacle*," the chief mate stated.

"I can see that," Bartlett replied. "Lock missiles on the nearest ship. Starboard and port, forward. Confirm."

"Missile lock confirmed," the weapons officer replied.

"Fire."

Cyclone missiles launched from both sides of the *Superior* and streamed toward the nearest enemy vessel. The four other Collective armada ships had closed distance and locked on the remaining two. Through the observation window, Bartlett watched the missiles swarming like angry hornets to their targets.

Then, all three enemy ships simply winked out of sight.

Bartlett slammed a fist on his chair arm.

"The counter!" he yelled. "What about our counter?"

"The gravity carrier has been active," the chief mate

confirmed. "It may not be working."

"Vessels reacquired," the second mate stated. "They've scattered . . ." He gave a range of coordinates.

"Rearm missiles and engage the closest target," Bartlett said, thinking that his aspirations to admiralty might have been slightly premature.

Inside the media control room, Striker had received messages from the *Harrier*, *Talon*, and *Death Rattle* as soon as they had skipped in. He immediately sent his programming adjustments to each ship, which they in turn downloaded to the remaining skip spheres that had been deployed earlier by Captain Fletcher.

Through the comm chatter, he pieced together that the Pack ships had been able to destroy a Collective vessel. Then, all three had been targeted by the remaining Collective craft. If his adjustments to the drones didn't work, this would very likely be the end of the mission for all of them . . .

He waited through seconds of tense silence. Then:

"This is Katz," the *Harrier* sub-captain reported. "It worked!"

Sub-Captain Bard of the *Talon* came on next. "Alive and kickin'."

Finally, Sub-Captain Auric said, "*Death Rattle* is still in play."

Striker whooped and pounded the nearest terminal in celebration. They might just make it out of this yet.

He glanced outside to see Braxx removing himself from the ruined Vulcan suit. It was a shame to have his heavy armor out of commission, but the *Skipjack* was momentarily able to target any autocars that came near while still protecting Aladhra and Kring's rear.

He shifted his gaze to Aladhra, who said a few more words, then raised her arm—the signal for Striker to broadcast the data he had uploaded. On the holotrons, her face was replaced by a timestamped holo-vid recording.

It was from back when the Old Man was young, an investigation conducted following the crash of the transport that had killed thirteen of Pindl Folk's classmates.

Striker had seen this footage once already, but he was still struck by it. The man chairing the review panel was instantly recognizable: General Carter Brawn, a soldier who would become the Collective's top military advisor, and bitter enemy to the rebels, in later years.

Striker looked outside once again. The spectators were long gone, but half of the holotrons still cut back and forth between crowds on the moon, Mars, Titan, Enceladus, and Dione. They all stood, silent, watching and waiting. An eerie silence prevailed in the Performance Center, broken only by the voices on the screens, their images partially obscured in the smoke of multiple wrecked cars.

"You've completed your investigation into the crash of transport *Destiny*," Brawn said on the holotrons. "Destroyed en route to Utopia Planitia, Mars, killing thirteen aboard."

"I have," the man sitting across from the panel answered. He was an older man, who had been unknown to Aladhra and not identified through Striker's research.

"And what are your findings?"

"The *Destiny* crash was a direct result of sabotage," the man replied.

CHAPTER 35

At the ISNN broadcasting station in Mars orbit, inside the main control room, Phil Morrow sat watching with a handful of others as the tight-beam broadcast from Earth came in.

The Ridgerunner woman he had met with had successfully liberated Dane Koros, with cameras rolling all the while. The entirety of the events had been relayed from ISNN headquarters throughout the system, and the reactions of the gathered crowds had been relayed as well. Now, the pirate woman was making accusations against Pindl Folk.

At this time, a call came through on Morrow's headset, a call from Collective Earth, explicitly stating that ISNN was to cease broadcasting immediately.

As Chief Broadcast Engineer, Morrow had arranged to be in the control room at this particular time, after the Ridgerunner woman had told him to do so—though she had not given him specifics regarding her plans.

Also as Chief Broadcast Engineer, Morrow had made sure he would be the one to answer any calls from the Collective.

"Copy that," he responded.

"Was that Collective Command?" the operations manager, Tully, asked.

"It was," Morrow answered.

"And?"

This was, potentially, a life-or-death decision for him, and he understood that one hundred percent. It was a point of no return. He had already betrayed the Collective, but at least there had remained some degree of plausible deniability. This there could be no denying this. He would be labeled a seditionist, and if he was captured, he would be tried and executed.

He looked to the screens that displayed the faces of those who watched from various points around the system: ordinary men, women, and children who had been kept in the dark for far too long. He thought once again of Tarsigh's final words to him:

"Be one of the good ones."

"Collective Command doesn't seem to be too worried," Morrow responded. "Keep broadcasting."

———◆———

Aladhra was still on the platform, watching the holotron footage. Kring was at her side.

"Key components of the *Destiny's* fusion drive system were compromised," the older man said.

"I see," Brawn answered. "And did your investigation point to any suspects?"

"Blood was found on one of the components," the man answered. "The blood belonged to a student, Pindl Folk."

"The sole survivor," one of the panelists put in.

"There was blood all over," Brawn argued. "It was, after all, a crash."

"The blood was on an *internal* component," the man answered. "One that remained in its housing even after the crash. Someone attempting to sabotage the components might very well cut themselves and leave blood behind."

"If this were done deliberately, how could Folk have known he would survive?" This was from the same woman who had spoken a moment ago.

"Folk's major is in mechanical engineering. He would know that parts of that class of ship are programmed to separate in the event of a crash," the man said. "Each contains safety measures to ensure a soft landing. The safety measures of the crew and passenger compartments failed. The safety measure for the engine room did not."

Aladhra looked to the holotrons showing crowd reactions across the system. Brows were furrowed. Expressions of doubt, denial, of dawning realization could be seen on their faces. Young Pindl Folk had always told rescuers that he crawled free of the passenger compartment. What the man in the vid was suggesting, of course, was that Folk had hidden in the engine room when he knew the crash was about to happen. What Aladhra had realized when she first viewed the proceedings—as she hoped the entire system now would—was that Brawn and the others on the panel had covered it up, probably called the evidence "inconclusive" and buried it for their own agendas and allegiances to Folk's powerful family. The so-called Miracle Boy was not just a fake; he was a murderer.

This was the smoking gun Tarsigh had found on the cube. As the cruiser returned to take her and Kring to the *Skipjack*, Aladhra wondered if it would be enough. Would it make a difference? Would it serve as a wake-up call? Would it chop the head off the snake? She looked once again to the holotrons cutting back and forth among the various crowds. People were looking up in confusion, then looking to each other.

This gave Aladhra hope.

The wail of autocar sirens blared, growing louder. Reinforcements on the way. She had insisted that the cruiser pick up Striker first, but it was time now to leave; most importantly, it was time to get everyone else to safety. Aladhra boarded the cruiser, daring one last glance behind. Braxx had re-entered the cargo container and been sent back to the *Skipjack*, a timed-detonation drone now hovering in the crate's place.

Within seconds, Aladhra and Kring were aboard the *Skipjack*. On the bridge, she updated herself on the progress of the *Harrier*, *Talon*, and *Death Rattle*. The Collective countermeasure had been thwarted, and her three ships had proven to be nearly impossible targets for the Collective armada to hit.

239

"Gungan, get me the *Harrier*," Aladhra ordered.

"On," Gungan replied.

"Have you identified Bartlett's ship?" she asked the *Harrier* captain, Katz.

They had. Coordinates for the *Superior* were sent. Aladhra looked to a nearby time display. Miraculously, there had been no significant delays to their timeline.

"Scan for other nearby Collective vessels," Aladhra ordered.

Kring answered from Aladhra's old station. There was one ship. He gave coordinates.

"We're in visual range?" Aladhra asked.

"Affirmative," Kring responded.

"Good," Aladhra said as she pulled up a tactical holo-display and turned to Findlay. "Set a collision course for the *Superior*," she ordered. "Half speed."

Captain Takashi eyed the bridge clock. It was time.

"Move us into Saturn orbit, maximum speed," he ordered the *Monolith* navigator. "Head-on to the equator."

They had been holding position just outside of Saturn's scanner range. The navigator complied now, thrusting the massive ship to a point just within Saturn traffic control but giving them an unobstructed path to the gas giant's equator.

The *Monolith* had been ordered to stay behind for a few reasons: first, Aladhra had wanted at least *one* ship from the Pack to survive, should things go south. Second, they had a finite number of drones, and skipping around three ships would be easier than wrangling four, especially one as big as the *Monolith*. Most important, however, was the reason that Takashi felt the most compunction over: before the operation, he had met with her and confided that the responsibility of being a captain weighed heavily on him. He had enjoyed being a Second; he believed that was his place. Since the death of Gordo, he had felt increasingly lost, unsure.

Takashi's reluctance had contributed to Aladhra's decision, but it had also aligned with the last reason the *Monolith* had remained behind: it was the only ship in the Pack capable of launching a Colossus-class missile, one of the only missiles in existence capable of obliterating an entire vessel with one strike.

The missile launch tube ran underneath, longitudinally from the vessel's bow to midships. The Colossus missile currently armed had been modified by Striker with Europan tech.

"Collective ships inbound," Takashi's second announced.

The sub-captain flicked his gaze once again to the clock. "Fire on my mark. Three . . . two . . . one. Mark!"

"Missile away," the second announced as the gargantuan projectile launched from the tube, hurtling toward the core of the planet, gaining speed as the gas giant's gravity drew it in.

"Shields up!" Takashi ordered. "Take us to open space and prepare to skip."

———◆———

Captain Bartlett stood just a meter away from the observation window. The Ridgerunners had been playing a game of cat and mouse, but the *Superior* had managed to locate and destroy at least one drone. Two of the armada ships currently had one of the pirate vessels flanked.

"The ship's rolling, sir," the second mate announced.

Bartlett squinted; the man was right. *Why*—and then it hit him. "Missiles armed? Which side?"

"Yes, port," the officer answered.

"They're going underneath! Look for a drone—"

But it was too late; the ship disappeared just as both Collective vessels loosed missiles. It reappeared far below, launching its own port-side missiles into the underbellies of both vessels.

Bartlett cried out in frustration. Then the Ridgerunner ship he was watching winked out of sight yet again. "Where'd it go?" the captain asked.

"Enemy vessels are no longer showing on scanners," the second mate relayed.

"Sir, we have an incoming video transmission," the communications officer announced.

"Pinpoint the source and lock coordinates. Accept the transmission," Bartlett said.

A flat-plane hologram appeared one meter in front of the captain's seat. The woman whose face appeared in the image was familiar, despite her makeup and change in hairstyle.

"Captain Bartlett. Do you remember me? You may not be aware . . . that after we captured your ship, I was the one who argued for the lives of you and your crew to be spared."

"Vessel approaching . . . from Earth," the second mate

said. "It's on a direct collision course with us."

"Shields? Weapons?" the chief mate said as he joined Bartlett.

"Shields are down, weapons not armed," the officer replied.

What the hell was this?

"Scan for drones in all directions," Bartlett ordered, "Anywhere within immediate missile range."

The woman on the screen continued, "That was a mistake. But I've been learning from my mistakes . . ."

"Nothing. Drones have moved out of range," the second mate said.

"Lower shields and fire every missile we've got," Bartlett commanded.

"All missiles fire, aye," the weapons officer responded.

"You've been living on borrowed time," the woman on the screen said.

"Enemy vessel increasing speed," the second mate informed.

The woman continued, "That time is up. Make no mistake: what's about to happen to you is revenge, plain and simple. For Tarsigh."

"Missile impact in 3, 2—"

"For my father," the woman said. The transmission ended.

"Enemy vessel has vanished," the second mate said. "Missiles aborted."

No no no.

"Missile! Enemy missile incoming!" the officer yelled. "Colossus, moving at—"

"Shields up!" Bartlett ordered.

Bartlett had a millisecond to register both his mistake and the fact that his immediate surroundings were being atomized before all thought and awareness simply ceased.

One instant Aladhra had been seeing the growing image of the *Superior* through the observation window; the next, she was looking at the surface of Saturn.

"Pull us up!" she ordered. The *Skipjack* shuddered as she fought Saturn's gravity. This had been the part of the plan Striker had tried to talk her out of; if they failed to escape the gas giant's gravitational pull, the ship would crumple under its pressure.

There was, however, a reason for this part of the plan. Not just the killing of Bartlett, not just revenge. She was trying to do something consequential for her crew—something to ensure that Tarsigh's sacrifice had truly not been in vain—but first, they had to survive.

The tremors grew more violent as the ship nosed into Saturn's atmosphere.

This was it, the final variable. All or nothing.

"Findlay!" Aladhra barked.

Her heart hammered against her chest. She couldn't tell whether they were resurfacing through the gas miasma or plunging deeper into it.

The obscured visibility lingered several tense seconds, until the shuddering subsided, bit by bit, and she could see stars once again as the *Skipjack* pulled free of Saturn's outer layer.

Aladhra let out a long, relieved breath. "Get us clear of the planet and prepare to skip," she said.

CHAPTER 36

Aladhra's assumption had been that the Collective would brand the recording a fake.

Much to her surprise, the new CEO of Collective Earth, Brenn Condon, had done no such thing.

What they did claim was that even before "allegations of wrongdoing" had surfaced, the Collective had been in the process of terminating Pindl Folk. As to what punishment might await the former executive, if any, that remained to be seen.

As far as the skip tech was concerned, from what Aladhra knew, the Pack had still managed to keep it from the Collective. All drones that had been left behind had since been swapped with the explosive "special drones," so the Pack would continue to have a leg up, an advantage she intended to maintain for as long as possible.

The most exciting development had come through the secured channels: word that the one-billion-chit bounty had been lifted. It had been the "bonus" Aladhra had hoped for in the killing of Bartlett: she had made sure the *Skipjack* was in view of a Collective ship in near-earth orbit—the *Synergy*, she later learned. The captain of that vessel had, as she hoped, witnessed the *Skipjack* racing toward Bartlett's ship *Superior*, a blur of motion, and the captain had later reported that the "Pack vessel had collided with the *Superior*, resulting in the decimation of both." The assumption on the Collective's part had been that Dane Koros had been killed, and that yet another command ship of the Pack had been destroyed. Which in turn had apparently been enough of a "win" for the suits to call off the bounty.

The bridge doors opened. Aladhra turned to see a cleaned up Dane Koros enter.

"Cruiser inbound," Jepps informed from his station. Then he, Findlay, Gungan, Striker, Braxx, and Kring all turned their attention to Koros.

"I can't thank you enough," the former captain said from the center of the command deck. "I wouldn't be alive if it weren't for you. All of you." He turned to Aladhra. "I was very sorry to hear about Tarsigh," he said. "I know I had kept my distance, but I thought it best. I knew if my crew and I were captured, the Collective would probe us. Still, I considered your captain a good friend, and a great man."

Aladhra nodded. "Yes, he was."

In the intervening silence, Koros added, "I guess I'm just

wondering what my place will be. How I'll fit in here. If you even want me here . . ."

Aladhra nodded for Koros to follow as she stepped over to the observation window. Soon the two of them were there, taking in Pack ships and empty space. "See that ship there?" she said, pointing to the *Monolith*.

"She's a beauty," Koros replied.

"She's yours if you want her," Aladhra said, smiling. "I know a pirate named Takashi who'd make a great Second."

Koros considered quietly for a moment, then decided: "That sounds perfect."

"Cruiser docked," Jepps announced.

Moments later, Aladhra, Kring, and Braxx stepped into the *Skipjack* meeting room, where Phil Morrow had already been escorted and seated. Aladhra sat at the table head. Kring sat across from Morrow, and Braxx remained standing.

"I, uh . . . I got away as soon as I could," Morrow said, glancing at Braxx nervously. "The Collective is no doubt on to the fact now that I helped you."

"And so what?" Aladhra said. "You came seeking asylum?"

"Not exactly. Well, I just—I thought that since I helped you out, did what you asked—"

Kring clenched his jaw. Braxx stood uncomfortably close. Aladhra simply stared at Morrow in response. Morrow waited anxiously.

Aladhra smacked his shoulder, making him jump. "We're just hassling you," she said, standing. "You're too easy."

Morrow smiled, relaxing. "There's something else," he said. Aladhra and Braxx waited. "I know that you have a lot of data, information that can be used against the Collective.

I have ideas, ways to go about doing that. I watched the people, you know, their reactions to the Folk vid . . . if the people can be coaxed a bit more, to question authority, then that's just the first step."

"To what?" Aladhra asked, intrigued.

"To *challenging* authority," Morrow said.

"Not bad," Aladhra replied. "Still, we'll need to toughen you up if you're gonna be one of us. You'll learn why it is we say, 'strength from within.'"

She cuffed him on the back of the head on her way out the door.

EPILOGUE

Condon awoke, staring at a blank ceiling. He turned his head; the room he found himself in was ornate. Luxurious.

But something was very, very wrong.

His body felt weak, frail beneath the covers. He moved slowly, pulling the fabric away . . . but the pajama-covered torso and legs he stared down at were not his, couldn't be his. The feet, while expertly pedicured, were old, unfamiliar. His entire being was unfamiliar.

The door to the room opened. Bullock strode in, eyeing him evenly, followed by . . .

Him.

He was looking at himself. "You're awake," his voice

said. Two Collective guards entered. "You were out for quite a while. We thought that might be the end."

His body walked over to stand next to the bed. "The fact that you're still alive is, I suppose, the good news. There is bad news, I'm sorry to say. You're under arrest. For murder."

He tried to speak, to respond. The voice that came out was barely a croak, which quickly evolved into a fit of coughing that had him clutching his burning chest.

The other him turned to the guards and said, "Leave us for a minute."

The guards complied.

"Funny how things work out," the other him said, pulling up a chair.

Condon struggled to sit up. There was a mirror on the wall opposite the foot of the bed.

Bullock came to stand next to the different him.

"We were going to just erase you . . ." the other him said.

Finally managing a sitting position, Condon looked in the mirror to see the Old Man staring back at him.

The different him—the hijacked him, Condon now understood—continued speaking: "Just say that Pindl Folk died quietly in his sleep. But then, when the attack happened . . . when they released the information, well, it all kind of worked out. With you living out your days in solitary confinement, it'll give the people a sense that at least some kind of justice was done."

The hijacker reached out, grasped Condon's thin wrist, and said, "Not just solitary . . . you'll be residing in another prison as well, won't you? The same prison I was confined to all of my life. But one that I'm afraid won't last for much longer."

The hijacker took in a deep breath, stood, and stretched. "I feel good. Better than I've felt in many, many long years. Thank you, for spending all those hours in the gym. Time had nearly caught up to me. But I did it. I managed to find a way out. After all, how many times did I tell you . . ."

The impostor leaned down and favored him with his own smile.

"Always have a backup."

ABOUT THE AUTHOR

Micky Neilson is a two-time *New York Times* bestselling author whose graphic novels *Ashbringer* (#2 on the list) and *Pearl of Pandaria* (#3) have both been published in six languages.

As one of the first writers at Blizzard Entertainment, he wrote the StarCraft novella "Uprising," as well as StarCraft short stories "Sector Six" and "Stealing Thunder." He also wrote the StarCraft digital comic *Nova: The Keep*. His memoir *Lost and Found: An Autobiography About Discovering Family* was published in 2016. He has also written a full-length horror novel, *The Turning*, and its prequel, *Whisper Lake*.

In 2017 Micky was tapped to write the comic book series *The Howling: Revenge of the Werewolf Queen,* a continuation of the beloved 1981 Joe Dante horror film *The Howling*. His most recent work is the *Call of Duty: WWII Field Manual*.